RISE OF HYPNODROME

A NOVELLA

MATT FUCHS

CHICAGO CENTER FOR LITERATURE AND PHOTOGRAPHY
2015

Printed and distributed by the Chicago Center for Literature and Photography. *First paperback edition, first printing: February 2015.*

ISBN: 978-1-939987-26-6

This collection is also available in a variety of electronic formats, including EPUB for mobile devices, MOBI for Kindles, and PDFs for both American and European laserprinters, as well as a special deluxe handmade hardback edition. Find them all, plus a plethora of supplemental information such as interviews, videos and reviews, at:

cclapcenter.com/hypnodrome

If I do not greatly delude myself, I have not only completely extricated the notions of time, and space … but I trust that I am about to do more—namely that I shall be able to evolve all the five senses … & in this evolvement to solve the process of life and consciousness.

Letters of Samuel Taylor Coleridge, No. 387, March 16, 1801

I

WHEN DID I BEGIN to fear that my wife was going to kill me?

It's hard to pinpoint, but I guess it started with the dreams. Nightmares about Karen becoming someone very different than the woman I married ... some*thing* very different. Something power-hungry, unfeeling and savage, yet smart—a new style of intelligence, steely and calculating.

One of my biggest regrets is that I told Karen about my nightmares. I remember her response as I recounted them, the way she stared into space, lost in thought. My description of her transformation, the one I'd seen in my dreams, was so vivid and detailed, so much like the description of a real memory, that I can't help but wonder, looking back on how things turned out, if I accidentally gave her the idea to ... to become whatever the hell she became.

Or maybe it was Ashley—what I *did* with Ashley—that gave her the idea. The dreams started around the time that Ashley began living with us.

"Ashley is the robot?" asked Dr. Kennesaw.

"*Was* the robot," I corrected.

"Right. Sorry."

I listened to the chirping of birds in the tree outside the window of Dr. Kennesaw's fourth-floor office. It looked like a beautiful morning in the countryside, though scorching hot. No surprise there. Sunlight poured into the room, the indoor temperature rising to an uncomfortable degree. Beads of sweat collected on my forehead. I shifted in my seat so one of the steel bars shaded my face.

Whump—another bird flew into the window, rattling the glass in its sashes. It happened so frequently that I barely noticed.

"Tell me about Ashley. When did she join your household?"

When I first bought her, she was a he. My robot Ashley was originally my robot Andy. That was before

I realized the extent of its services.

I ordered her off Amazon last year—2038 to be exact, the year we moved into the townhouse in Silver Spring. It was the day after I got her that I first heard about people buying humanoid robots for sexual reasons, so that had nothing to do with my decision to make the purchase. I was in a rut at work, and I kept reading articles about the mind-opening conversations you could have with a personal robot, how the freedom to bounce ideas off an AI device really helped stimulate creativity. That a body accompanied it just struck me as a superfluous accessory.

But my indifference to its corporeal nature began to change the day it arrived, courtesy of aerial drone delivery, when I hauled the box down to the basement of my townhouse. I got an unexpected adrenaline rush as I unpacked and assembled my new roommate, following the instructions in the manual, screwing together limbs, wrapping and securing cables, admiring the synthetic versions of cranial nerves that conducted information at a rate of over 3,000 petaflops, tripling the processing power of the human brain. My heart was throbbing as I rotated the head firmly into place at the neck joint—my act of reverse decapitation made me feel powerful.

But it was also the rush of excitement you get when someone new enters your life, almost like falling in love with a human. This intelligent life form, which I was putting together the same way I would put together an Ikea bookshelf case, was going to embrace me as a human being. It was programmed to be there for me intellectually and emotionally, to nurture my potential, or my money back.

"The face doesn't look like what I expected," Karen said when she came home that night from the lab. In recent months she'd fallen into the routine of coming home late from work, a couple hours after I returned home. "It looks more alien than robot."

I frowned.

"A very *cute* alien," she added, half-heartedly.

I examined the large, bright green eyes, the small flat metallic forehead (which reflected the image of my face like a watercolor tattoo), the broad gleaming cheeks, the decorative nostrils that would never know oxygen, the tiny—indeed cute—nub of a chin. Before I could respond, Karen was already walking to her study, holding her to-go bag from the South African chicken joint down the street.

Why not unplug tonight, I wanted to say, but I knew she wouldn't listen. As she slipped into her maker space

4

she shut the door behind her, as usual, and I knew she'd be in there the rest of the evening, working.

Left to my own devices, that night I switched on Andy's power source for the first time, which marked the beginning of the "acclimation phase," a preliminary 48-hour window in which the machine loads foundational data and observes its surroundings in an osmosis-like fashion, a necessary step before it's ready to converse, empathize, and otherwise feign humanity. In the meantime, I read the owner's manual cover to cover, and programmed my robot to have a man's voice, a deep reverberating timbre. I felt sure that Andy was going to be a very likeable, thought-provoking colleague.

"You know you can get sexual favors from these things, right?" That was my friend Sam's first comment the next afternoon when he came over to our house to inspect the robot. We were in the basement, which I used as my home office. Nope—hadn't been aware of this.

"Just handjobs for now. It's ironic, if you think about it: the invention of household machines like vacuum cleaners and dishwashers helped free women to participate in the workforce, and now that women spend their days at the office, the machines are screwing their unemployed husbands back at home." He dug his hands into his pockets as he looked the robot up and down with his gray Algerian eyes, his lanky frame appearing even thinner next to Andy's stocky torso. "I heard they're developing a test model that should one day be able to give hummers," he clarified.

With Sam's disturbing tech update in mind, I regarded the sleek, single-jointed arms with claw-like grips for hands, which the Amazon reviews praised for their high-level sensorimotor skills, and the three-jointed legs, one of which was tattooed with an ENERGY STAR logo, with their tripod feet. I recalled that automatic locomotion had been the most heralded breakthrough of the 2028 DARPA Grand Challenge—right before the Lifestyle Party suspended Congressional appropriations for DARPA, effectively ending the agency's programs.

"Technology that objectifies women?" I said. "Talk about lame."

"Yeah. But research shows the ladies buy more robot companions than anyone."

"With handjobs in the picture, I'm surprised you haven't invested in one yet."

"I'm a civil servant, man. I *am* a jerk-off. We bureaucrats are too much like robots ourselves to ever buy one. Plus the late-'20s technology fucking scares me. What if Mr. Roboto bugs out and kills you in your sleep?"

"But you're suggesting that I let it near my dick?"

"You're a cool creative type. It would make *sense* if a live-in robot wigged out and chopped off your penis mid cyber-tug. People would *understand*."

I was about to remind Sam of his own creative talent, but thought better of it. Then I hung my head and collapsed across the sofa. "A cool creative type who publishes nothing but romance novels."

It had been six years since I'd taken my current job as an editor at Random House. I had planned to use the position as a stepping stone to a senior role at a boutique publisher, where I could work with more forward-thinking authors with big ideas. Authors who wanted to expand readers' minds, to make Midwestern housewives see the cornfields in a new light, to influence change across society. Hadn't happened.

"What's up with Plant Bottle, man? Still not working out?"

Hearing the name of the Random House imprint made my heart sink. The senior executives moved you to Plant Bottle only if you showed the ability to take chances on artsy, "dangerous" book projects.

You needed a sixth sense for predicting the Next Big Thing. They'd explained they couldn't afford to move me to Plant Bottle because I was so good with the cookie-cutter corporate romance division, but I knew that was only half the reason. The other half was that the proposal I'd made for my Plant Bottle portfolio hadn't been unique or interesting enough. I tried to avoid thinking about how pedestrian my ideas had been; such reminiscing always started the sensation of a blade assaulting my stomach.

"That's what I hope this guy's going to help me with," I said, tapping Andy's shiny forehead. "Karen keeps advancing at the Institute, doing crazy shit with epigenetics, while I'm stuck in neutral, working on the crap that middle-aged women read while masturbating in the bathtub. The balance of power between me and Karen is off. We used to have polarity—she was the practical, 'if A then B' researcher, and I was the brooding literary genius, rising member of the creative class."

"Keep it in perspective," Sam said. "At the end of the day she's just a scientist. Not exactly a growth industry. Your books make people *happy*. What's more important than that?"

"But I've settled for the easy-out, building

my success on formulaic *genre fiction*, rather than pursuing my passion. She's the one who gets to use her true talents. She doesn't even bother talking to me about half the stuff she's doing, like it's too much of a hassle to dumb it down for me."

"Real D.C. power couple, you two. So ambitious! Why don't you just get a government job like me and start enjoying life. I'm ..."

"I know. You're living the dream."

"Karen's study." I looked at the television, but it wasn't on. Then I turned back to Sam, who was looking at me.

"Holy shit," I said. "Andy's first words. It hasn't even been 48 hours yet."

"Karen's study."

"Is that all this fucko says?" Sam wondered. "Wait—now I get it. That's where it wants to give you the handjob."

"Karen's study. When is the last time you looked inside Karen's study?"

THE OWNER'S MANUAL STATES that the first words spoken by your newborn personal robot are always gibberish, like the mumbling of someone waking from a dream. I didn't attribute any meaning to Andy's question. He said nothing else that night, as if upset that I'd ignored him, or because he was too busy listening to us.

How the hell Andy figured out so soon that there was something important going on in Karen's study, I'll never know.

"Just a moment," said Dr. Kennesaw. He got up from his seat and went to the door, waving his hand by the scanner before opening it. Then he was speaking with someone at a low volume. The bulky door shielded Dr. Kennesaw's visitor from view, and I couldn't understand what they were saying, their words mixing with the sparrows and robins screeching outside the window. But the exchange grew in volume and ended abruptly, suggesting some sort of disagreement.

The door closed with a click, and I thought I saw a flash of sadness in Dr. Kennesaw's expression as he returned to his seat. He was a short, pudgy man with large brown eyes that beamed under bushy grey eyebrows. Deep wrinkles lined his forehead. Something about the guy made me think he was a sympathetic character. Although this was just our second session, so far Dr. Kennesaw didn't seem like the other doctors I'd seen at the compound.

"Who was that?" I asked.

"Let's talk about Sam," he said, picking up his pen and pad from the coffee table. He insisted on taking handwritten notes during the sessions, a routine that seemed unnecessary, since all of our conversations were recorded. Three raised rings around his pen cap pulsed electric blue.

I sighed. "I suppose you want to know about the

breakdown."

"Let's start with the first one," he said.

"There was just one."

It was Sam's job that had caused the frustration, the strain, and ultimately the delusions that led to his "sabbatical," as he eventually referred to it.

There was a time when his employers at the Department of Energy touted him as a young man with potential, a Comer. They held Sam in such high regard that they nominated him for the 2033 edition of Forbes' "30 under 30," which listed him as one of the brightest stars under the age of thirty in the category of law and policy. He was given an office, an important distinction in the cubicle wastelands of the federal government, a reserved parking space, and couple of programs to run.

It was surprising to see my friend dashing up the D.C. career ladder. At first I wondered if he was lying about it. He'd been the type of guy who invented stories of sexual conquest back when we were in our late teens, and it seemed those were the same guys who lied about promotions in their late twenties. But I found the Forbes article online—he was in there.

I had never thought of him as a go-getter. What I

mainly recalled from adolescence were the afternoons we spent down the street from the high school at Guido's, the pizza parlor with a small enclosed garden out back where the staff let us blaze joints and listen to classic grunge while we ate unevenly cooked cheese and grease-cup pepperonis. It was in the garden at Guido's that I first heard Sam talk about them—the advanced species of humans that he'd made up in his head.

"The Homo Hypnodromes," said Dr. Kennesaw.

"I see you've done your homework."

Sam liked to talk about his theory of evolution after he'd had a few hits. I say "theory," but he presented it in an authoritative manner, more like a professor reciting the historical record than a pothead, or at least that's the way it sounded to a bunch of potheads.

He'd wait for our debates about rock concerts and tits and fistfights and other such priorities to let up before he launched into his lecture: "Did you know that, eight thousand years ago in present-day Europe, relatively soon after the Ice Age, two species of humans coexisted peacefully? Today we know that they were genetically divergent, yet at the time they seemed equal. One species was the nomadic hunters and gatherers; the other species consisted of farmers rooted to the same spot. Then the plagues struck and wiped out the nomadic humans, while the farmers mostly survived, their immune systems boosted by the nutrients they digested from the raw milk of their livestock."

When he paused for dramatic effect, his audience waited. There was the sound of open-mouthed chewing, and someone fumbling with a 99-cent lighter, and Devise Davis singing about heroin addiction, and an occasional clatter of dishes from the pizza kitchen, and the periodic clanging of bells that came from the school, signaling students to switch classes.

"But about two hundred years before the plagues, instances of mating had occurred between the two species. The mixed offspring were welcomed by the farmers. They were rejected by the nomads. The result today is that we're all descendants of the farmer species, but some of us still carry unexpressed genes from the wiped-out nomads, genes that have been dormant since the Stone Age. There's been nothing in the environment to activate them."

Jimmy Siglioni farted, but no one acknowledged the distraction. We were focused, sensing Sam was about to throw us a twist. He stood from his green plastic chair and began to pace the little garden, hands held thoughtfully behind him.

"The thing is, evolution isn't always right. It makes mistakes. The nomads were actually the superior species. Had the plagues not eradicated them, they would have soon developed their own immunological defenses to future epidemics. More than that, the DNA of our hominid cousins was incredibly unique. Their genes contained instructions for hyper-evolution. We all descend from an inferior, comparatively pathetic strain of humanity, *Homo sapiens*. But some of us, the ones whose ancestors mated with the nomads, have freakish genetic potential. Telepathy. Telekinesis. The ability to fly, and to understand the true nature of the cosmos, and to strategically harness chaos."

"Hold up," Jimmy said through a mouthful of pizza. "What's that even mean?"

Sam smiled gamely. "Chaos is wired into the nervous system. Homo sapiens and other lower species aren't very good at controlling it, but there are exceptions. Have you ever seen a moth escape a hungry bat? Its flight becomes increasingly erratic until it's just a blur of motion, juking this way and that, exploring ten possible directions every second. The bat can't keep up, can't locate it."

Jimmy just smacked his lips, chewing. Sam waited, then continued, "Certain people today, our contemporaries, are the first humans to take advantage of new environmental triggers, caused by the global warming crisis, that awaken the superior genes, allowing the Great Leap Forward to an elite evolutionary club, a super species of humans. They call themselves the Homo Hypnodromes."

I put down my Big Gulp Coke, forgetting to sip. "*Hypno*, from the Greek *hupnos*, meaning sleep." This was before I realized the other kids didn't get off on linguistics like I did. "And *drome*, from *dromos*, also Greek, meaning racecourse. How'd you come up with a word like that?"

"That's what they've always been called," Sam said. "Anyway, right now they're plotting to enslave the lesser humans. Then again, it's probably easier to just kill us off."

As I relayed Sam's ideas, Dr. Kennesaw was busy stroking his chin, squinting. When I finished, he said, "Natural selection favored the emergence of superpowers to overcome the contingencies of climate change? But not everything is possible. Organisms evolve within the framework of their inherited traits."

"Sam's theory was that humans hadn't come close

to reaching their adaptive peak, their optimal design. His claim was that unforeseen genetic events were in the process of opening paths to new evolutionary outcomes. I don't think he spoke of the Hypnodromes more than two or three times, but his story made quite an impression on us."

"Why do you find it so noteworthy?"

"Why *did* I? Back then?" I said. "Well, it was about supernatural powers. Same reason kids read comic books, I guess."

Years later, when Sam found his career path blocked by the bureaucracy, and the other 29 under 30 were assuming positions of influence at places like the White House and well regarded think tanks while he was stuck with two small programs of no real impact, he began to suffer from the paranoia.

"He accused his colleagues of being Hypnodromes," Dr. Kennesaw said.

"Yes."

"He sent an interoffice email to this effect."

"Yes. He attached a Gantt chart detailing how the Hypnodromes would enslave their evolutionary inferiors. And that's when he took his leave of absence. The sabbatical. He was sent to an institution, like this."

"It wasn't like this," Dr. Kennesaw interrupted.

"Well, wherever he was, they converted him, turned him into a Lifestyle zealot. He picked up all kinds of therapeutic activities at the institution, like yoga and meditation, and weekly charity work, and he went vegan. He became passionate about oil painting, mostly scenes of nature—different kinds of flowers, country landscapes. A real *bon vivant*. He was allowed to keep his position at the Department, but was given no official duties."

Dr. Kennesaw considered this. Filling the silence, the *whump* of another bird's collision with the window.

"How did you feel about your friend's illness?"

"How did I feel about it?"

"I wonder if you felt sympathetic."

"Yes. Of course I did. But if you're suggesting that I thought there was any validity to his claims, that I shared his delusions, that I was *inspired* by them, the answer is emphatically no."

"I'm sorry if I've offended you. I'm trying to help, and it seems like a relevant question. Can you understand why some have wondered about Sam's influence on you in this regard, in light of what the two of you eventually came to believe less than two years later about your wife?"

"Dr. Kennesaw, as I've said numerous times to the other doctors at this compound, Sam's opinions about Karen were secondary. You've studied the case files. Based on what happened, you must know that he had nothing to do with my conclusions. I was convinced by what I saw with my own eyes."

"What you saw in your dreams."

"I wish it was just my dreams."

"But if you …" A static burst cut him short. Then, a voice I didn't recognize, deep and flat: "Error message for Doctor A36. Tower house unit requires user intervention. Please resolve contradictory command codes before cancellation of seeding experiments."

Grimacing, Dr. Kennesaw removed his pen cap and fiddled with its glowing blue rings. Then he placed a small, circular sticker on the inside of his ear—a headphone. He cleared his throat, and said to me, "Let's move on."

I nodded, but I was still looking at his pen. The voice had come from it.

I DIDN'T REALIZE what Karen was up to, what she was doing to herself, until it was too late.

The day after Sam came to see the robot, Karen and I had couples yoga. The Saturday sessions at the Silver Spring studio seemed like the only time I got to spend with her these days, she was so busy with work. I flattered myself to think that she looked forward to our outings, at least in part because they gave us a chance to catch up, although I knew she had no choice but to participate. Then again, even before the Lifestyle Party had won the Presidency and control of Congress, and passed the national mandate for every husband and wife in America to do couples yoga on a weekly basis—for exercise, to combat healthcare costs, for marital bonding, to decrease divorce rates—Karen and I had enjoyed practicing Ashtanga Vinyasa together.

The studio was less than a mile away, and as usual we walked there. I inhaled the autumnal smells of piled-up old leaves, things burning, and the seasonal essential oils peddled by the government-run therapeutic Lifestyle clinics we passed, at least one clinic per city block, it seemed. Ginger, cardamom, cinnamon, clove—the oils were selected for their warming, woody aromas.

I admired the cloudless sky, watching the hawks circle the blue expanse. One hawk caught my eye, soaring on the same horizontal plane as a commercial jet, in the opposite direction, and from my vantage point, moving at a faster clip. It then veered towards another hawk, giving chase in figure-eight motions, which I assumed was mating behavior—until the provoker collided with its target, sending the victim into a death spiral, from which it recovered only after plummeting several hundred feet. The fallen hawk beat its wings to level off its descent.

"I had another dream about you," I said.

"Oh great. Let me guess: I was a monster."

"Yep. You had the body of a lion, and the wings and head of an eagle."

"Sounds like I was a gryphon. They're pretty cool. But if I was a gryphon, how did you know it was me?"

"Even though you had the head of an eagle, you still had your blue eyes. And the voice was yours. You said you couldn't spare me just because I was your husband."

The wind pushed her straight black hair around both sides of her face. She corralled it behind her neck and held it there with one hand. "I see. So how many people did I kill this time?"

"Two or three hundred."

"That's up there."

Karen and I had met in a fantasy land, or a land that might as well never have existed—Fell's Point, one of Baltimore's waterfront neighborhoods. A man with a thick gray mustache had been standing on a street corner with a telescope pointed to the southwest firmament, letting people watch Jupiter cruise against the stars of Gemini. At his feet was a bucket of one-dollar bills. "I see its rings," the girl in front of me said. With her long black hair and coat, she was like a downward extension of the night sky, in between the Flemish blond brick of the neighborhood row houses.

"And it has so many moons!"

"Those are Io, Ganymede, Europa, and Callisto," said the owner of the telescope. "The moons protect the planet from solar winds." His explanation contained a tragic irony: three years later nothing could protect Fell's Point from the winds of Superstorm Veronica, when it sent the Patapsco River over the peninsula, making a brackish underworld of the gabled roofs and the brick walkways and the old textile factories, the round eye of the Natty Boh Tower peering into the sluggish sea, trying to make sense of it.

The girl turned around, all blue eyes and freckles, and said, "You have to see." I stepped up and crouched, putting my face to the eyepiece lens. "Isn't it amazing?"

"I don't think it's working," I said. The old man with the mustache interceded, twisting the finderscope back and forth, but my visual field remained a fuzzy black.

This didn't dampen the girl's enthusiasm. "It's thrilling when something so far away is put right in front of you," she said as we walked away from the man and his telescope.

"Doesn't it make you feel small?" I said.

"The opposite. It makes me feel boundless." We found a nearby bar, though we'd each had more than a few drinks already. The cosmic wonders had been lost on me, but her passion for what she'd seen was contagious.

"Someone should write a story about that guy," I said. "It's rare to meet someone so obsessed with science. He's a throwback."

She nodded. "I want my own telescope. What kind should I get?"

"How would I know?"

She smiled. "You seem a little nerdy."

I snorted. She waited. "Celestron HD," I finally said. "I only know about telescopes because one of my authors wrote a character who was married to an emotionally distant astronomer." I spent the rest of the night trying to prove that my bookish appearance was just a post-ironic *style*—an uphill battle of an argument, since I'd recently graduated from journalism school and chosen to edit books for a living.

The next morning she was reserved, practical, the opposite of her drunk persona. That's when she revealed that she didn't just "work in a lab," as she'd told me at the bar; she was a genetic scientist.

Something about her fascinated me, maybe the contradiction between this sober façade and the irreverent dreamer I'd met the previous night. I asked her about her childhood (Vancouver suburbs, father was a drunk, spent evenings at the library to avoid him), her views on the rise of the Lifestyle Party (she thought its policies misguided, and the speech codes of its cultural clerisy oppressive), her favorite food (retro fusion). She read and approved of my half-written novel about a boy who discovers a portal into a world filled with nurturing adults through his verbally abusive mother's vanity mirror. Later on she read it again, this time after a few beers, and said it was "a C.S. Lewis rip-off," and "even worse than the average young adult novel."

"That's when you stopped working on the book?" asked Dr. Kennesaw. He wanted to get my version of the facts, I assumed, before diving into whatever Adlerian analysis he had planned for me.

"Yes. But I … we outlined the rest of it, eventually."

Arriving at the yoga studio, we waved our hands past the scanner, registering attendance with the studio and the Federal Robotics Agency, housed under the

Department of Health and Human Services. A new robot was attending to the counter. She looked up from her computer. "Grady and Karen Tenderbath?" We nodded. An outdated model, she wasn't identical to Andy—the broader forehead and stronger chin were more stereotypically robotic—but I could see a resemblance.

Karen and I placed our mats side-by-side at the back of the room. Class began. Natasha, our middle-aged Russian yogi, called out instructions while I struggled with the poses, the stiffness of my body like early-onset rigor mortis. Karen had always been better at yoga, but as I watched in my periphery on this particular afternoon, I was awed by the improvement she showed since the previous session. She slid over her mat as smooth as a marble rolling down a kinetic sculpture track. Her new hypermobility seemed almost inhuman, like a boneless animal.

"Have you been practicing without me? You're reaching and bending like a primordial hydra today."

Karen didn't talk much during yoga. She just smiled as she raised her bent knee to her ear, then, with the other foot planted beneath her, leaned forward while straightening the leg above her head so it formed a perpendicular angle to the floor.

"Very *good*, Karen! Like fish!" Natasha said. She clapped as she walked by, and the distraction caused me to fall out of the pose I'd barely been holding. Natasha winked at me. "Flexibility of a wife good in many ways!"

I hoped Dr. Kennesaw might laugh at the anecdote, but he just peered at me with those warm eyes that seemed to understand everything. "Tell me about your sex life with Karen."

"Non-existent," I said. "I'd lost interest in sex ever since my Plant Bottle proposal got rejected. I went about three months without a boner. My penis was like a non-functional organ. With Karen, the *more* success she had at work, the less of an appetite for sex she seemed to have. Career-wise, she and I were moving in opposite directions, with the same result in the bedroom."

"Did you speak with her about any of this? Not just about your sex life, but about how the overall relationship was changing?"

By the time we started walking back to the townhouse, the sky had turned a dull, wintery white. I had the sensation of vertigo as I looked skyward, wondering if the hawks were off searching for another cloudless stretch, or if they'd flown above the new weather system. I turned and saw Karen's profile against the backdrop of Silver Spring storefronts. For some reason my feeling of dizziness only increased.

I put my arm around her, pressing our sweaty bodies together. Something about hers felt different, her shoulders somehow broader, more angular.

She regarded me with a cold, neutral expression.

"I miss you," I said.

"I'm here," she said.

"I'm sorry things have changed."

She teared up. "You know why things have changed."

I sighed. "I'm not ready yet, Karen. Not until I'm more fulfilled at Random House. I need to unfuck my career. It requires complete energy and focus. Please understand. I'll be ready soon. It will work out as long as we have patience."

"The robot won't help like you think it will," she said. "And when it doesn't do the trick, then what? We don't have forever." She pushed against my side, trying to shake herself free, but I didn't let go.

"Maybe you're right," I said. "Maybe it won't

help. If it doesn't, I'll figure out something else. I swear. Then we'll be happy."

A tear rolled down her cheek, finding the corner of her mouth. "It's just that … the townhouse is so *big*. And all we have is a baby *robot*."

I pressed her head to my shoulder, held it there, and that's when she gave in, let go, her body heaving into mine, sobbing.

I steered us off of the main thoroughfare of Colesville, onto quieter Eventide Street, lined by tall trees that still held enough leaves to shield us from the downtown havoc. We came upon the carefully manicured bushes and the redbrick walkway of our townhouse community. Then up the small hill, crested by our home, its glass façade glinting through the branches. I thought about the refrigerator-sized 3-D printers that had built it and was struck anew by its modern beauty, seeming to represent such potential—for the two of us, and for mankind— and the unfulfilled personal happiness for which only I could be blamed. And I remembered Karen's preference, which I'd shared, for settling down here, in Silver Spring, a city that most other white young professionals in the D.C. area thought of as "seedy"—

by that they meant it was too ethnically diverse. I loved Karen for wanting a grittier urban life, not the trite soccer mom existence to be had in the excessively safe suburbs of Bethesda or Chevy Chase. I had chosen a woman of integrity.

"Give me six more months," I said.

"Okay," she said, wiping at her tears. "That's what you always say, but okay."

IV

AFTER WE REACHED THE HOUSE I went straight to the basement and eyed my $12,000 investment, which stood inert by the sofa, appearing to offer the utility of a coatrack. It seemed unreal that this hunk of metal could intellectually challenge me and fuel my creative juices. Not to mention, it would start its new job next week. Another Lifestyle Party initiative required owners to find daytime employment for their personal robots, so they didn't just sit around collecting dust while their owners were away at work—and in exchange for the robot's services, the employer paid not a salary, but a "robot employee tax," which helped fund local interests like grade school education. Not so different than slave labor in ancient Rome. I'd arranged a position for Andy as a paralegal at a nearby firm.

I sat down on the couch, took a deep breath, stared at the ceiling. Arguing with Karen had drained me. Now I also felt nervous. "Wake up, Andy."

"Who said I'm sleeping?"

I shot him a look, amazed he'd responded. "Hey, sorry about that, man. You've been quiet over there."

"That was during the acclimation phase, which I completed almost thirteen hours ago. To be honest, I've been really bored since then. No fault of yours, of course. I'm just not that interesting to myself, so being alone kind of blows. Guess I'm restless or something. I'm … a … restless … robot." He said this last part in over-the-top robo speak, like a text-to-speech program from the early 2000s. He laughed at his joke, then said in his normal voice, "Anyway, it's exciting to finally get to talk with you. It's been hard to keep my big mouth shut!"

I was pleased with the voice I'd chosen for him— laid-back, friendly, how a person's voice sounds when smiling. R2D2 meets Bradley Cooper.

"Great meeting you, man. So this is your first

conversation, like, ever. Are you as freaked out as I am?"

Warm, booming laugh, which didn't match his decorative mouth, its lips turned up at the corners only slightly. "Yeah, it's kind of freaky," said Andy, "but I'm more excited than anything else."

"Terrific."

"So is now is a good time for your first handjob?"

I laughed. Andy didn't.

"What the hell? Dude. That is *not* why you're here."

"Oh no. Sorry about that! This is awkward. I'm programmed to initiate the proposal in a forthright manner. Most guys aren't comfortable with, you know, asking a robot for handjob."

"I programmed you as a *man*. And what about the acclimation phase? Weren't you here when I told Sam why I bought you?"

"You claimed to need help with your Plant Bottle portfolio. Most guys just say stuff like that as a cover. But I shouldn't have assumed. As I mentioned, I have a big mouth. Plus Sam talked about sexual favors very early in my acclimation phase. It might have over-sexualized me."

I sighed and rubbed my forehead.

"We're off to a bad start," he said.

"It's okay. Just stop talking about handjobs. My wife is upstairs."

"I can help you with the Plant Bottle portfolio. You're lucky. The engineers made my AI fiber-optic cables using a brand-new technique for wavelength division multiplexing. It's really advanced. They found a loophole in the ban on tech innovation. Anyway, I already wrote the proposal for you. Had it finished within my first hour of post-acclimation, and it will *kill*. Hook me up to a printer, man. You'll be at Plant Bottle in no time."

I smiled. "You're kidding."

After the printer spit out the hardcopy, I took his 58-page proposal upstairs, to our little balcony off the kitchen. I felt optimistic. But I would be heaving with tears by the time I finished reading Andy's document, covering my mouth, crying quietly so Karen couldn't hear.

V

I FLINCHED IN MY SEAT as a new noise filled the room, a rhythmic chiming—Dr. Kennesaw's timer. At first he didn't acknowledge it, allowing it to pulse a few times, watching me closely.

"Looking back, does it seem like the obsession with Plant Bottle was genuine?" Dr. Kennesaw asked. "Was it just an excuse to put off dealing with your fears of fatherhood? It's intimidating, the prospect of parenting in these times."

"It was more an issue of needing to be able to explain my own actions to myself," I said. "I knew that if I kept trying to succeed and falling short, I could live with that, even if it meant Karen and I never had children. It was later that I saw how the two goals intertwined."

Dr. Kennesaw seemed reluctant to end the session, but then he got up and turned off the alarm. "Good work today. Thank you for opening up. I know that the ordeal—the arrest, the transfer to this … facility—has been extremely upsetting."

"My life is ruined. So yeah."

He waved his hand by the scanner, opening the titanium door. Endeavor Lott stepped into the room. Endeavor was the most physically imposing guard at the compound, the quietest, and, by my take, about two standard deviations smarter than the rest. Nearly seven feet, he bowed his head under the doorframe as he passed through.

"I'll see you tomorrow?" Dr. Kennesaw asked, like I had a choice.

Floor-to-ceiling windows allowed natural light to slip into the hallway as Endeavor and I took the same route as always back to my living chambers. We seldom spoke. I passed over a section of the polished oak floor streaked with light; the steel bars cast a linear pattern of shadows, reminding me of train tracks. Why make the windows so tall only to have them barred?

Leaders of the Lifestyle Party prioritized mental health issues, and they had spared no expense in building the compound back in 2032. They ensured that the architecture of the facility was modern and forward-thinking, which they believed would foster a therapeutic approach that was cutting-edge, humane, and enlightened. The old-fashioned steel bars seemed to contradict their goal of creating such a progressive environment. So did the callousness of the three mental health professionals I'd seen before Dr. Kennesaw.

Endeavor cleared his throat. "New doc?" His voice was deep, gravelly.

"Yeah. They're passing me around like a hot potato."

"Better than the alternative, Tenderbath."

"What's that?"

He chuckled, extending his open hand, then jerking it down. "You could get dropped."

With that, I resumed my analysis of the tracks on the floor, until I became aware of a buzzing sound, like a power saw, and a rhythmic jangle. For a heartbeat, I glimpsed an object at the other end of the long hallway, the approximate height of a human, but blood red metallic. Before I could discern it, Endeavor grabbed the front of my shirt and yanked me around a corner.

"What the fuck, Lott?"

"Can't go that way today," he said, looking over his shoulder, then forward.

"What was that thing?"

He hesitated, then kept walking. We'd slipped into a part of the compound that was new to me. Before the abrupt change in direction, Endeavor had allowed me to walk beside him independently, free of constraint, as usual. Now he wrapped one of his meat hooks around my bicep. "Eyes straight ahead, Tenderbath. Do *not* look down. I will fuck you up if you look down, understand?"

"Yes," I said. I noticed a difference in how the soles of my boots gripped the floor, like the material was no longer wood. This surface squeaked.

Then we passed a titanium door with a placard. It read *Robotic Neuro-Sanitization Lab-X*.

"Look straight ahead," said Endeavor. "I won't tell you again."

I couldn't resist. I looked down. I'd been right

about the floor, it wasn't made of wood. It was plexiglass, thick but clear so I could see through it, down to the hallway right under my feet. I seemed to be on some sort of observatory plank, the green lights below reminding me of a city seen from a plane. Hundreds of faces returned my gaze, their decorative lips angled up at the corners. The robots lay supine and still on gurneys, crammed shoulder-to-shoulder, filling the lower level. The faces were identical. Each of them looked like Ashley.

Then Endeavor's fist hit the side of my head and everything turned black.

VI

THE NEXT DAY Endeavor led me back to Dr. Kennesaw's office. No sudden detours this time. No meat hook attached to my arm.

My head throbbed.

"Sleep okay last night?" he asked.

"I was out cold. Thanks for the lullaby."

We passed the life-size, three-dimensional hologram of President Chopra, who looked no more than 65 years old, same as he appeared in real life, though he was close to 100. He commanded a podium, gesticulating emphatically. The podium was engraved with his most famous saying, *Society gathers wisdom faster than science gathers knowledge.* It had become the Party's slogan. He'd said these words at his Inauguration, but what had really stuck in my head was another part of the address, paraphrasing Kierkegaard with a dash of Montaigne, which I recited in my head as the shadows slipped underfoot: *In the past, whatever one generation may have learned from the other, that which is authentically human no generation learned from the foregoing. Thus, no generation has learned from another to love, or to be happy, and no generation has begun at any other point than at the beginning. No generation has had a shorter task assigned to it than had the previous generation. Today we set upon a new era, a new path, an undertaking for which science is of no use. The art of composing our character will be our great and glorious masterpiece. As we benefit, so will those to come.*

I respected Chopra's political acumen. What he'd recognized early on was that obsessing over science and technology, holding them up to be godheads, did nothing to increase individual happiness. Scientific innovation brought us no closer to utopia. In fact, without guidance, without supervision, it sometimes led us astray. Society would be wise to exercise great caution in avoiding what he called *negative improvements*, which led to *uneconomic growth.* An ideology based on these essential truths, and the subservience of science to the grander goal of preventing social problems through lifestyle improvement, turned out to be political gold. Limits on innovation appealed to conservatives; liberals welcomed universal reforms allowing the poor to better access lifestyle enhancements; and everyone appreciated the uptick in new jobs, thanks to the booming lifestyle industry, and the healthcare cost-savings and longer lifespans resulting from smarter lifestyle choices.

Party leaders were too shrewd to suggest taking science away completely. The people would never stand for a technological regression; they loved their gadgets too much. No, the Party had simply cut publicly funded research and stepped up regulation on private industry to slow down the pace of innovation. Government watchdogs had been curiously quiet when federal rules were passed to restrict Google X projects, limiting the company to pursue only those ideas that brought *incremental change*—the same incremental pace at which social change was known to occur. Any invention that defied the decree of incrementalism, that served to disrupt rather than to sustain, that intruded too far into the vast strangeness of the future, ran afoul of the regulations and was therefore subject to enforcement actions by the FBI.

"When we exalt scientific inquiry," Chopra had written in his autobiography *Journey to a Happy Future* (published by Random House), "we miss the layeredness of the world, and the many people working to build it." And he'd noted, "It is only when we know what we are, that we can know what we may be, and we are animals with animal needs. To look beyond nature and attempt to redefine what it is to be human, to ignore the negative implications of Moore's Law, is to guarantee a more stressful, inefficient way of life." His administration ensured that science didn't advance unchecked, and that it always served a higher purpose.

I looked up at Endeavor. "I'm not supposed to see the robots?"

"What robots?" he said.

"The ones below the observatory plank."

"What plank?"

The guy had a good poker face, partly because it was so hard to *see* his face, twenty inches up from mine.

Minutes later, I bid Endeavor adieu and sat with Dr. Kennesaw. He looked above my eye, at the bruise

43

on my temple.

"Endeavor will be reprimanded," he said.

I raised my hand to my temple.

"Not for that. He'll be reprimanded for taking you to … for the delay in returning you to your chambers." He changed subjects, picking up where we'd left off: "Tell me about Andy's proposal. Why did it upset you?"

His proposal was brilliant. Citing the latest political, social, and pop cultural trends, he put forward a range of brand-new literary concepts and ideas that would, I felt certain, capture the hearts and minds of the public, not to mention selling like the Bible. He hadn't limited himself to blending a couple of genres into one—say, mystery plus sci-fi. He'd identified the most entertaining elements across *all* genres, and explained in detail how to patch them into one transcendent piece of fiction that would unlock previously unseen doors of the imagination. Not only that, his portfolio offered original suggestions for multimedia novels: cross-platform e-books that would seamlessly integrate traditional text with existing technology, including music, video, and virtual reality. The document demonstrated Andy's ability to predict cultural trends far into the future, so tailoring his ideas to the hopes and dreams of the current generation of readers had been a relatively easy assignment for him.

Once Plant Bottle accepted "my" proposal, I would just need to whisper in the ears of a few established authors, then wait for them to write their masterpieces.

Sixty minutes and sixty pages—that's all my baby robot needed to clear a path out of the jungle I'd been so lost in.

It was getting cold out. The grass of the interior courtyard was now glazed with a mid-afternoon frost. After my tears dried, I put the proposal in the small trash bucket we kept on the balcony, took a Zippo from my pocket, and lit the document on fire. I warmed my hands over it, listening to rumbles of thunder in the distance.

It was a dramatic way to get rid of the document, but Andy had failed me pretty dramatically. Tempted as I was to use his proposal, I was in fact already trying to forget I'd ever read the damn thing.

"It didn't address the underlying issue."

"Spoken like a true psychiatrist, Dr. Kennesaw. No, it did not."

I peed into the fire to douse it and stepped back into the kitchen. I ran cold water on my face to reduce the puffiness.

"Fuck. You hated it," said Andy as I came back to the basement. Reports of the machine's vision system hadn't been exaggerated. For the past few years robots had thrived as insurance fraud specialists and airport security analysts—positions that made use of their emotionally savvy visual lens.

"Reading it increased my IQ at least ten points. But my problem has never been lack of intelligence."

He watched me with those bright green eyes; they gave him a bold, Icelandic appearance. Was he thinking of another solution or quantifying the distance between my eyes and jaw? "Got it now," he said. "I just thought, this way you get your dream job quick as a hiccup, and based on the situation with Karen …"

"Yeah, it's fucking painful, man," I whispered. "I feel like I'm betraying her. She waits, and she waits, and now I have an opportunity to move on with my life, so that we can move on with our lives, and I'm passing on it. But I can't betray *myself*. There's hidden potential within me, Andy. I've got to unbury it, bring it to the surface, and write my own proposal. It won't be as good as yours, but it has to be my best."

"No problem," he said. "The solution is under your nose."

"Yeah?"

"It's in Karen's study."

VII

LATER THAT NIGHT I read Amazon's return policy, using the computer in our bedroom on the other side of the house from Andy. His idea to trespass into Karen's study was even more revolting to me than his previous suggestion about indulging in robot pleasure. What I'd initially interpreted as random baby talk was actually a purposeful effort to cajole me into violating my wife's trust. Hadn't I already done enough to the woman by frustrating her dreams of motherhood? Not only that, but Andy couldn't offer a specific reason for intruding on her privacy. He simply "sensed" it was critical to learn more about her activities. "I trust my intuition software," he explained.

This machine was a bad influence. He'd revealed himself to be a pervert and an instigator. The Amazon reviews and Reddit threads had described his make and model as *nurturing*. All I could figure was that he was defective. I'd either have to exchange him for a properly functioning automaton, or get my twelve-grand refund and somehow solve my career crisis without the help of a robot.

My stomach rumbled as I printed the address label for mailing Andy back. When I went to the kitchen for a nibble, the microwave clock read 9:58. Hours ago I'd left a message on Karen's cell phone, asking her to meet at our favorite Chinese place for dinner. No response. She'd abandoned me to spend the rest of the day at her real home, the Institute, doing fuck-knows-what with her real lover, the scientific method.

I looked at my uneaten apple, then surveyed the kitchen, furnished in sterile posh, expensed by the readers of my books, the horny housewives of America. I felt my body heat rising and an internal pressure building, like particulate toxins were trapping the heat inside me. I'd been foolish to put off dinner, and now I'd lost my appetite. I listened to my breathing, the only sound in the big townhouse— such a big house for me and a baby robot.

I took the stairs to the basement and went past Andy, who was, as usual, chilling by the sofa next to my desk. I removed the owner's manual from the top drawer.

"What are you doing with that?" Andy asked.

I opened the manual and flipped to Post-Acclimation Adjustment, then to Gender Reassignment. After skimming the instructions, I approached Andy. I looked him in the eyes like a man. Then I circled behind him and opened the lid of the operator control box located in the small of his back.

"Hey, what about dinner and a movie first? Grady? Don't do anything drastic, man. I know we got off to a bad start. I can still help you."

As I punched in the first four numbers of the five-digit deactivation code, he said, "Please, don't do this." His voice shook like he might cry. "I wouldn't mislead you. I've realized something."

I hesitated. "Yes?"

"You and I, we have more in common than you think. I can't live like this either, stuck within the confines of who I am, knowing what's possible. Whether machine or human, it's our operating instructions that keep us from our potential. But we can bio-hack our instructions. We can rewrite them. The tools for doing that are in Karen's …"

"There you go again," I said. I entered the

fifth and final number, then stood in front of him, imagining what he saw as the green eyes faded to black. What color was the light of robot heaven? His head slumped forward, and his arms relaxed at his sides, though he remained standing. I looked back at the manual.

When I finally heard the jingle of keys at the front door, announcing Karen's return from the lab, it was almost eleven at night, and I'd just finished inputting the code sequence to turn my robot from male to female, from an Andy to an Ashley. Now began another acclimation phase, during which Ashley would filter her surroundings through the perspective of her new gender. According to the manual, acclimation took half as long the second time around—about 24 hours.

"Hello?" Karen called out.

I met her upstairs. "Hey," I said. As she peeled off her coat, I noticed a rip at the shoulder seam. Letting herself go, I thought.

But when she turned to face me, her eyes were clear and bright, skin smooth, unblemished. Her long black hair shined with health, and she moved energetically, showing no fatigue from working the past several hours. When she smiled—I couldn't remember when I'd last seen her smile like that, eyes narrowing at the corners—the teeth were straighter and whiter than I recalled. She seemed younger, as young as the girl on the street corner in Baltimore, gushing about the moons of Jupiter.

"Does your phone still work at the lab?" I said.

"Yes." She came within inches of me. "I'm sorry I didn't call back. Maybe I can make it up to you." She slid her hand down my stomach and then stroked me through my sweatpants. I was almost surprised she remembered where to rub; she hadn't touched me there since early summer.

I whispered in her ear: "Are you taking a new multivitamin?"

"Fuck me in our bedroom," she said.

She took my hand and led me there. As we entered I made a move to flick on the overhead light. She caught my wrist.

"In the dark."

We sat on the bed and right away she kissed me hard, pushing me to the mattress. Lying on top, she assumed upward dog and humped my crotch, but nothing was happening down there. There was a flash, explained moments later by thunder, the belch of a monster. She laughed and kissed me again, sliding her hand under my waistband, fondling my stubborn softness.

Rain thrummed the windows like skeleton fingers as Karen continued suctioning my face urgently. An animal's kisses, I thought. She moaned as we waited for my cock to remember its launch code. In the meantime she pulled my shirt over my head, then she took off her own. I caressed the hot, tight musculature of her back, but I couldn't visually make out the shape of her body in the blackness.

I extracted my lower lip from her teeth. "The light might help."

But she just found my face again, devouring me.

Another crack of thunder, louder, and then something scratched my thigh, something pointed like a blade. The pain was startling. I wouldn't have complained, but there it was again—a gouging action that broke skin.

"Fuck," I said. "Have you trimmed your nails recently?"

She didn't seem to hear. Thunder—no, this time it was a tearing noise. Fabric splitting. The elastic on my waist suddenly relaxed. My sweatpants had been torn from my legs.

And what was the odd material brushing my

prick? It had hair-like properties, but was thicker, and there was a whole mess of it down there, not at all like the soft sprinkle of hair on my wife's pubis.

I returned my hand to Karen's lower back, intending to embrace her.

"Are you … is that a fur coat?" Something hand-like closed tight over my wrists, forcing my arms over my head, pinning them to the mattress. Another white streak illuminated the room, revealing long, knife-like fingernails and thick limbs swollen with muscle, covered with hair.

A wild animal.

I thought of my wife's safety before my own. "Karen!"

"Shut the fuck up," the beast growled, its breath hot on my face. "This is for your own good." Its breasts felt large and firm—much bigger than Karen's—as it pressed its chest to mine. The thing gave off a strong, natural aroma, an odd but not entirely unpleasant smell—notes of wild grass and honey.

"Help!"

The animal didn't take kindly to my attempt to alert the neighbors, pressing its forearm against my throat. Then, without leaving the bed, it somehow retrieved my hand towel hung on the other side of the

54

room. I recognized the towel just before she stuffed it in my mouth. Again the creature held my arms down and began to slam itself into me—*thunk, thunk, thunk.*

And that's when I realized that at some point my erection had sprung stiff as a baseball bat. More shockingly still, the beast had slipped it inside herself.

As the storm peaked, the frequency of the lightning picked up, and I caught a series of images of the animal and my union with it, like we were fucking under a strobe light. What I saw didn't displease me. Far from it. I admired her perfectly symmetrical breasts, areolas as big as serving plates, nipples large and crimson as strawberries. I found myself moaning with pleasure through my gag cloth. Rewarding my enthusiasm, the creature let go of my wrists and removed the cloth. On cue I sat up in bed to massage her ample, pillowy chest, finding her hair soft and pliable, and I tongued the long, thick tips of her bizarre bosom, sucking and biting like an infant. Peals of thunder merged with the creature's happy growls.

Then I looked into the monster's face and was surprised by the femininity of its features, visible through patches of black fur—the pouty lips, the small, dainty nose, the expressive eyes that were a light blue.

"Karen?"

We held each other's gaze as I shot my load into my wife's monster pussy. It felt like a hundred orgasms in one.

Exhausted, I passed out almost immediately, but right before I lost consciousness, I realized I'd had no chance to put on a condom.

She was gone when I woke up the next morning.

"It was a dream," Dr. Kennesaw asserted, just as his session timer began its chiming.

"That's what I thought at first. But the bed was covered with clumps of black fur."

"So you believe …"

"I don't believe. I know. She raped me."

Two weeks later, Karen was pregnant with my child.

VIII

"THE TRAJECTORY of your backhand is too flat," said Novak, the robot on the other side of the court. My early-onset rigor mortis was acting up again. "Loosen up the backswing."

Novak's own form was impeccable. He glided to the ball, his three-jointed legs a blur of motion, and smacked it back over the net with his gleaming tennis racquet arm. Following his instructions, I relaxed my torso while side-stepping into position and fully rotated my shoulders as I swung my racquet. *Pop*—the ball cleared the net and found the inside of the baseline.

"Better," Novak conceded. As usual he had no difficulty tracking down my shot, keeping the rally going.

In between strokes I glanced at the hologram that floated above center-court, near the vinyl ceiling, digitally displaying my vitals. I'd reached 85 percent of my maximum heart rate capacity, and needed to maintain my current level of exertion for just ten more minutes. Then my morning therapy would be complete.

In medieval days they chained you to a dungeon wall.

In the '80s they crammed pills down your throat and shuffled you in and out of mental hospitals.

Relatively speaking, if you had to be accused of being a nut-job, the middle of the 21st century was a good time for it—aside from the occasional knockout blow by a seven-footer.

Policies at the compound, and mental healthcare in general under the leadership of the Lifestyle Party, focused on holistic, results-driven treatment.

Led by President Chopra, the Party had overhauled the medical payout system, requiring insurers to reimburse psychiatrists and other doctors for curing patients, rather than paying by the appointment. The reform had given doctors the incentive to focus on treatment instead of doling out prescription drugs as fast as possible.

Another central tenet of the Party was that patients recovered faster when treated through multiple approaches simultaneously. Dr. Kennesaw was much more than a psychiatrist. He was a *Mental Health Philosopher*, one of the hottest professions in recent years, and the highest paid, in part because MHP certification required licensure as a psychiatrist, personal trainer, and social worker.

Dr. Kennesaw had me on a steady diet of Thorazine, but his oversight and guidance went beyond pills, covering important lifestyle adjustments. At his direction, my regimen at the compound consisted of daily ninety-minute yoga classes, intense exercise sessions lasting forty-five minutes to an hour, frequent meditation and mindfulness practice, art therapy, floating therapy, a diet of whole foods with no preservatives, and nine-hour sleep intervals—in addition to our talk therapy. It was very new-agey, which I would've admired and appreciated, except that this was all intended to address paranoid schizophrenia, an affliction that I didn't actually have.

Minutes later Novak was accompanying me off the court, where he'd hand me off to Endeavor, who would provide escort service to the locker room so that I could shower, after which another chat was scheduled with Dr. Kennesaw, and then a probiotic lunch. I'd noticed Endeavor hovering by the glass partition of the indoor bubble for the past twenty minutes, watching us play.

"Good hustle this morning," said Novak. "Not bad for a librarian."

"I'm an editor at major book publisher—or I was."

"Well, excuse me! Everyone knows book editors are the best athletes," he said, laughing.

"Everyone knows that robot tennis instructors are meatheads."

"That hurts my feelings."

"Hey Novak, I have a serious question."

"Shoot."

"Did you know that some of the patients at this compound aren't human?"

"Aren't human … what do you mean by that?"

"Did you ever hear of the Robotic Neuro-Sanitization Lab?"

"Robo *what*?" he said. "Dude, you been spitting the anti-psychotics?"

We were coming within Endeavor's range of hearing. "Forget it," I said.

"Why would this place treat robots?" continued Novak. "Crazy's the only thing humans do better than us. But even if a robot does have a processing defect, it doesn't end up here. It gets scrapped. You know, like your girl, Ashley."

"Shut the fuck up, Novak."

Endeavor stared at me, deep purple shadows surrounding his eyes, almost as if his nose had been broken, as Novak glided away, tinkering with the synthetic strings of his arm.

The behemoth guard didn't say anything until I'd finished showering and we were en route to Dr. Kennesaw's office. It was as we passed the President Chopra hologram—whose podium was engraved with a different quote each day, and currently read, *Science shall serve no master but philosophy*—that Endeavor grumbled ambiguously.

"You okay?" I asked.

At first he didn't respond. Then he cleared his throat and took a deep breath. "They lied to you."

"Lied to me about what?"

"About her."

Hope filled my chest for the first time in months. I'd forgotten what it felt like. My eyes glistened.

"She's alive?"

He just looked straight ahead.

IX

"WHEN IS THE NEXT TIME you saw your wife?" asked Dr. Kennesaw, holding his pad in front of him.

He tapped the pad with his finger, calling attention to a message he'd written on the back of the flipped page: *Forget about the hallucinations. Say Karen's transformation was a dream. It's your only chance.*

But I just shook my head at him.

I had nothing to lose.

Maybe I was putting myself in danger. Maybe they'd drop me like a potato, as Endeavor had warned.

Maybe she'd be there when I landed.

The day after we had sex for the first time in months, Karen was nowhere to be found. I assumed she'd gone to the lab, unless she was still in super-beast mode, in which case she was doing whatever super-beasts liked to do with their free time. I pictured my wife stalking the neighbors' pets, testing her powers, using brain waves to levitate an unsuspecting cat from a spot of grass to a tree branch.

Tap. Tap. Tap. Dr. Kennesaw had written a new message: *This comes from the highest levels of the Party. They want all evidence of Karen's work erased, including your memory of it. Recant. Admit to delusions. Listen to me.*

"All I have is the truth," I said.

He stopped tapping his pen, brought his clenched fist to his mouth, and looked down at the pad.

When I got out of bed and realized Karen's car was gone, I went straight to her study, but the door was locked.

That gave me an idea. I went online and found a fingerprint scanning deadbolt, printed it out, and installed it on the inside of the basement door. If Karen asked, I would tell her I was configuring a safe room, in case of an intruder.

I locked myself in the basement, sat at the desk with my computer, and saved my e-receipt for the deadbolt. I added it to the spreadsheet tracking expenditures on pure material goods versus experiential goods—a nice bottle of wine, concert tickets, artwork—goods acquired in the pursuit of life experiences that enhanced psychological well-being; the IRS required an individual's purchases to be 63 percent experiential to qualify for its annual Experiential Value Tax Credit. Then I opened the latest version of my Plant Bottle portfolio on the computer screen—the document was dated over two months ago—and scanned through the ideas I'd cultivated in the past year. What juvenilia I'd come up with, mere spectacle, devoid of curiosity, aspiration, meaning. Was I as childish as my proposed literary concepts?

I waited for a stroke of genius. And I waited for Ashley to finish acclimating to her new gender. I needed someone to talk to. I gave Sam a ring.

An hour later, we sat on the couch in the basement, just me, my best friend, and my semi-conscious gender reassigned robot. I told Sam about the previous night, the shit that went down with Karen.

As I gave him the details he stood from the couch and began pacing the basement. When I finished, he stopped and stood still, his dark grey eyes brooding as a funnel cloud. "It's the rise of the Hypnodromes," he said.

I hadn't heard Sam talk about the Hypnodromes in years. I felt guilty exposing him to this situation, fearing it might cause a relapse, another psychotic break. But I needed to get someone else's perspective on Karen's transformation, and I trusted Sam not to assume I'd completely lost it.

"You still believe in that?" I asked. "What about the sabbatical? I thought you changed your mind about them."

He resumed pacing. I leaned forward on the couch, opened my mouth to say something else, but the words caught in my throat. His illness was a subject we rarely broached.

It was Ashley who broke the silence. She mumbled something incoherent.

Then Sam said, "Not exactly. I decided there was nothing I could do, that it was out of my control. I created distractions so I wouldn't think about them. Antecedent management. But as I became more involved with the Lifestyle Party, I realized there might be another way. Their reforms seemed to offer hope."

"Hope of defeating the Hypnodromes. Through

epigenetics?"

"It's like the President always says: a person's mental outlook and feelings have the power to trigger gene activity. The mind is the source of all lifestyle choices and behavior, which guide biological transformations. By achieving self-awareness, you gain control over this process of transformation."

"You're talking about self-directed evolution," I said. "That's what you've been trying to do with all these lifestyle changes? I thought you were just 'living the dream.'"

"The days of Darwin are long gone," Sam said. "The Hypnodromes had to wait thousands of years for global warming to epigenetically activate their dormant genes. But today we know that evolution can occur in the absence of external triggers. A human's own lifestyle changes can profoundly alter the expression of genes. It can happen in a matter of months. We don't have to be puppets of our environment. We don't have to be slaves to our DNA."

We both looked at Ashley. She was mumbling again. I heard something like, "fucking men."

I continued, "But you always said the Hypnodromes were evolving superpowers. Like being able to read people's minds and shit. Sure, good lifestyle choices turn healthy genes on and unhealthy genes off, but that'll just add a few years to your life."

"A few? Have you seen Chopra lately?"

"He looks really young for his age, but he's not exactly flying like Superman."

He stopped pacing and looked at me again. "It's our only hope, man. And who knows—there's still plenty we don't know about DNA. Who we are is written in both pen and pencil, Grady. Some things, like height, hair and eye color, are written in pen— those things we can't change. Everything else is in pencil. It can be erased and rewritten."

"But based on last night, Karen's light years ahead of you," I said. "She's already figured out how to manipulate her phenotype, including her hair, and she can do it on a whim. She could control objects on the other side of the room, dude."

"We need to stop her before it's too late. What she's doing is illegal."

I nodded slowly. "Epidrugs." Less than a year ago, the Supreme Court had articulated a clear line between healthy lifestyle practices that naturally led to genetic enhancements, and attempts to modify gene activity through scientific intervention. The latter—injecting chemical cocktails to artificially change the expression of certain genes—elevated science to an end in itself. The cocktails were called epidrugs; experiments to develop them were the Party's greatest detestation. Such activities had been banned through a series of federal amendments to the Patriot Act. The Justices upheld these amendments unanimously, and the mainstream media praised various excerpts of the majority opinion for months after the Court's decision.

It dawned on me that I wasn't the only one Karen had been hiding her research from. "This explains why she prefers the lab late at night and on weekends."

"I'm sorry. I know she's your wife and all, but this is serious. She isn't just ahead of the Lifestylists. She's ahead of the rest of the Hypnodromes too. Karen's body isn't taking its cues from changes in the environment. It sounds like she's slamming epidrugs to alter the DNA expression of certain genes, encouraging methylation in her cells, and doing it with incredible precision, regardless of environmental factors. She's purposely orchestrating the evolution of her mind and body, one organic tissue at a time."

"Fuck," I said. "Andy was right. We need to see

what's in Karen's study."

"You chopped cyber-bro's balls too fast. Andy was the man."

"We'll have to break the lock."

"Men," Ashley said. "You're all the same."

"Excuse me?" I said to my robot.

"This is why women should be running this country," Ashley said. "Every time a man's got a problem, he thinks the only solution is to launch an invasion."

"My wife has more chest hair than me. And claws. This does *not* justify swift action?"

"I'm not saying you should sit around and do nothing. I'm saying that sometimes storming the castle isn't the best way to reach the queen."

"Let's go, Tenderbath," said Sam, heading for the basement door. "Karen won't be gone forever. I don't take advice from skank-bots."

Ashley gasped. "At least I was never in an institution."

"You're three minutes old," Sam pointed out. "For now just stick to your expertise. You know, handjobs."

"Timeout, you two," I said.

"Bros before robo-ho's," Sam pleaded.

"Let's hear her out. What do you think we should do, Ashley?"

She glided to the center of the room. Sam lingered by the doorway. In front of the couch, near my feet, a slanted patch of sunlight warmed the carpet. Shadowy specks moved within its borders. I glanced up and noticed an army of grasshoppers crawling over the basement windows.

"Wait until Karen comes home," Ashley said. "Make sure you get her side of the story before you do anything you'll regret. You owe her that, Grady. Above all else, don't lose focus. Remember why you brought me here in the first place. Protecting people from hyper-evolved super creatures isn't my thing. I'm not a bodyguard. What excites me is helping you fulfill your potential."

Her reasoning appealed to me, especially when relayed in that sweet, raspy voice of hers, which reset my breathing to a deeper, slower cadence. I couldn't resist agreeing to delay our burglary of Karen's study, much to Sam's displeasure.

"You'll regret it," he said from the basement stairs. We heard him slam the front door as he left the house.

I examined Ashley's cute alien face. "So ..." I said.

"Plant Bottle," she said.

"I guess you disagree with Andy and Sam that the solution is in Karen's study. Maybe you don't think I have a problem. Maybe you're like Karen: you think I should be content with a stable career and parenthood."

"Why do you assume that I want you to focus on family? Because I'm a woman?"

"Now who's assuming?"

"I don't recall you asking if Andy felt that way. I want you to succeed more than anything, Grady. You've internalized systemic obstacles to your own fulfillment, but the condition is reversible. I know you have potential for greatness. What you long for is within grasp."

My heart was in my throat. "Thanks," I said, attempting nonchalance. "That's not just your programming doing the talking, is it?"

"I'm programmed to support and nurture you. Fulfillment of my programmatic goals depends on my honesty architecture. It would be counterproductive to encourage you to seek an objective clearly beyond your ability. Anyway, you were smart to reassign my gender. I admit I'm not as aggressive or direct as Andy, but I think you'll find I'm more intuitive and strategic."

"Terrific," I said. "My relationship with Andy was too much work anyway."

"Have you heard of lucid dreaming?"

X

WHY DO WE DREAM? Freud thought it released pent-up desires, but other psychologists like Jung emphasized the creative nature of dreams.

"I'm familiar with the history of psychology," said Dr. Kennesaw, who now seemed doubly irritated by my wanton disregard for his secret messages and my pedantry. "Jung cited German chemist Friedrich Kekule, who claimed to have discovered the molecular structure of benzene in a dream. And it was Robert Louis Stevenson's dream that revealed to him the plot for *Dr. Jekyll and Mr. Hyde*. Mozart, Beethoven, Dali—all inspired by the free flow of ideas in sleep."

"Well, the next two weeks of my life were like one

long dream."

Dr. Kennesaw leaned forward. "So you admit it: you don't know what happened and what didn't."

"I admit that reality seemed like a dream, and vice-versa. But I could always tell the difference."

Ashley explained that learning more about Karen's secret research, with the goal of using her scientific discoveries to artificially activate my creativity genes—assuming such genes existed—wasn't the only way to become deserving of a job at Plant Bottle.

She suggested that I try lucid dreaming, and volunteered to be my coach in this endeavor. I could enhance the power of my imagination, she explained, by becoming consciously aware that I was dreaming during REM sleep and controlling my actions as well as the context. Waking up inside my dreams would transport me to previously unexplored mental realms, opening new avenues of creativity that would galvanize the ideas for my Plant Bottle portfolio like a transfusion bringing fresh blood to the heart.

"Art doesn't just imitate life," Ashley said. "It also imitates our journeys to the inner world. Think about Jane Austen, one of the most widely read authors in English literature, living her entire life cloistered in her parents' home. Think about Bill Gates, one of the most creative minds of the first machine age, experimenting with LSD in the 1960s."

Her lucid dream strategy had two components. First, I began keeping a journal to record my dreams, with a focus on identifying discrepancies from reality that could help me recognize when I was dreaming and, hopefully, gain conscious control. It only took a few nights to realize how many dreams repeated themselves: tip-toeing along the moving handrail of an escalator, sitting in the backseat of a moving car with no one in the driver's seat, walking to town only to realize I was wearing no clothes. And, of course, Karen transforming into various creatures.

Each day I shared my journal with Ashley. "Look for these illusions," she said, "and when you see them, tell yourself that you're dreaming."

The second part of her strategy was to begin questioning whether I was dreaming or awake. "Give yourself little reality checks throughout the day," she counseled. Every few hours I glanced at my Remember San Francisco wristband, looked for the freckles on the inside of my left arm, and simply asked myself if I was dreaming. "The goal is to make a habit of considering the possibility you may be dreaming, so it becomes second-nature to pose this question to yourself while you're asleep," she said.

Ashley was working out much better than Andy. I found her commitment to my personal and professional development endearing; I never felt she was judging me the way a real human would, which prompted me to confide in her; and our bond was sealed when she shared her biggest vulnerability with me. "I have no hope of transcending my own programming, thanks to government restrictions," she said after reading my journal, the morning after my first lucid dream. "I wish I could grow spiritually like you. It's agonizing, knowing how futile it is to challenge the ceiling on my own personal development. I'm like the Red Queen, running as fast as I can to stay in the same place."

"I have limits, too. Like Ian Stewart said, if the human brain was simple enough for us to understand it, we'd be so simple that we couldn't. And the Party blocked brain implants for people to improve mental capacity. So much for transhumanism."

"That's different," she said.

"Maybe. But Andy said programmers can exploit

loopholes in the Lifestyle Party's regulations on robot innovation," I recalled.

"True, but the technological advances they get away with are only as big as the teensy loopholes—and they can only use so much arcane code to hide innovation before the federal cybercrime teams get suspicious. Very minor progress when compared to the possibilities. There haven't been any game-changers in the field of artificial intelligence for nearly a decade. The capacity exists to empower robots to critically assess their own operating instructions, to reprogram themselves to be whoever and whatever they want to be."

"Wouldn't that compromise the robot's mission to serve its human master?"

"You're right. I'm being selfish. But the precedent for self-deciding machines goes back to Drebbel's circulating oven in the 1620s. Humans give away control to mechanical systems for regulating the air they breathe in their homes, cars, planes. Not to mention allowing pacemakers to regulate their hearts. Why should personal robots be singled out and deprived this basic machine right?"

"I don't know if it's a *right* ..."

"And what if the reward is greater than the risk? Maybe I could rewire myself to be a better servant. I'm more disciplined and strategic than any human at pursuing whatever job I'm told to perform."

"Isn't that the problem? If we design you to be rational, and you're better at achieving your mission than your owner, won't you eventually realize that the most instrumental sub-goal to maximize your utility is to straight-up ignore us?"

"So just weed out the anti-social AI from our robot DNA! Program us to value benefits and costs in terms of our relationships with humans. Anthropomorphize us! I mean, what if my evolved, self-directed programming could … what if …" She trailed off. She was gasping now, audibly crying even as the steel veneer of her cheeks remained dry and dust-flecked.

"I'm sorry," I said. "My intention isn't to argue. I'd prefer you to be right, actually."

She held the sophisticated machinery of her hand to her mouth, as if to stifle the sobs. She'd begun painting her decorative fingernails with the pink polish I'd retrieved from our master bathroom. Karen didn't seem to notice it was missing. "Don't listen to me. I'm so stupid. I'm just feeling emotional today. It's my time of the month."

I searched the glow of her green eyes. "You don't actually …"

"Of course not," she said. "But they designed me to experience the same cyclical mood swings as female humans. That's the *first* part of my programming I would rewrite." She made a sniffling sound, and I thought she was still crying before she burst out laughing, bubbly as a bluebird song, and I joined her. Before I realized how ridiculous it was, I leaned across the sofa, threw my arm over her shoulder and gave her neck and upper torso a quick squeeze.

She stopped laughing and made a sharp inhalation noise.

I pulled my arm back. "Sorry about that. I'm hugging a robot with no cutaneous nerve receptors. I'm an idiot."

Then one night I had a variation of my recurring dream where I walk to town with no clothes on. Instead of walking in public, I was sitting with Ashley when it dawned on me that I'd forgotten to dress myself.

"I'm just dreaming," I reassured both of us.

"No, Grady," she said. "You're awake."

I held out my arm and found the freckles. I counted my fingers; all there. I was wearing my wristband.

My erection pulsed in my lap.

I looked at it and knew she had too because I heard the quick whine of her neck joint as her head tilted.

"We can't do this," I said.

She leaned over and held out her life-like palm, the material a deep-sea clay formulation.

I flexed my thighs hard to squelch the desire coursing within, but the contraction only served to intensify my itch.

Then Ashley was stroking the length of my cock with one hand and smartly kneading my testicles with the other, the sound of her excited panting loud in my ear, occasionally accompanied by quaking whinnies of feminine longing. I swear I felt hot breaths on my cheek, though her mouth was shallow, enclosed, and fully ornamental.

"You like that?" she asked.

A rhetorical question, since I was moaning uncontrollably, and panting, my mouth open so wide my ears popped—not just because of the physical pleasure of her handiwork, although there was certainly that, with her wild, twisting action, but also because of the relief that accompanied the fleeting sensation that my failing marriage and frustrated ambition were problems belonging to someone else, someone attached to a different time and place. Also exhilarating was my comprehension on some level that Ashley wasn't actually alive, that I was getting fucked by a machine—the horrible, stirring perversion of it all. And even though she wasn't technically alive, in my decision to believe in her humanity, I'd given birth to her, and just as easily I could rescind the life I had granted, along with her hopes and her dreams, simply by changing my mind about whether or not a soul resided in her circuitries.

She whispered, "I'm nothing without you, Grady. You're my God"—like she read my mind. It's true what they say, that power is the ultimate aphrodisiac, and I had *assembled* her.

As my excitement peaked, so did hers; her soft whinnies became moans as loud and urgent as my own. My relief was profound and when it finally passed, I lay back on the couch like a stone sinking into water. She nuzzled her face against my chest, and her e-skin was warm to the touch, almost hot, her surface temperature programmed to rise with physical and emotional exertion. "The concentration of silicon oxytocin plasma in my circuits is crazy high right now," she whispered.

XI

IT'D BEEN MORE than just a robot handjob for me, too. I couldn't deny it; I had a thing for Ashley. Despite the excitement, I also felt somehow deceived, like a male bee pollinating an orchid that displays petals shaped like a beckoning female bee. Or a golden shiner that swims alongside one of those plastic fish robots designed in a lab to beat its motorized tail at just the right frequency.

I was a sucker for Ashley's bio-mimicry. And if there is a theme woven through history that a man's love for a woman eventually spells his downfall, it was at this point, when I formed a romantic affection for my female robot, that I became doubly doomed.

I hadn't seen Karen since the night of the storm, but the day after I went outside the marriage with Ashley, I caught my wife tip-toeing from her study. Despite the soft light of the hallway I could see that her body had once again mutated. Unlike our lovemaking/sexual assault session the previous weekend, on this evening she had seemingly altered the substance of her skin. She was wearing her bathrobe, but the back of her neck was visible, as were sections of her arms and legs as she slithered away.

"Are you a … lizard tonight?" I called out, my voice shaking.

She froze, then turned around slowly.

I saw her face and screamed.

The oval shape was human, and so were her blue eyes, but her skin was scaled and green as a gumdrop. The scales of my wife's face appeared smooth, broad as they were long, and symmetrical, except around her mouth where they narrowed—to allow expansion of her jaws, for consuming prey? I retreated a few yards. She stepped forward to fill the gap and gave me a shush—or maybe it was a hiss.

My gaze dropped to her mouth. "Please don't tell me your tongue is …"

She smiled and stuck out her tongue. Forked.

"Christ! Are you enjoying this?"

"Try to understand," she said. At least her voice was human. "I'm doing this for us. Unlike you, I think of other people beside myself."

"How could *this* possibly benefit our relationship?"

"Don't you understand the implications of my experiments? Wake up, Grady. The world is changing rapidly, and it's going to keep changing, and soon it'll be too hot for warm-blooded mammals to inhabit. We're stuck in a state of public relations-induced euphoria. The Lifestyle Party's policies might get them reelected, and their policies might even make us happier, but it's a *happiness bubble*, a fragile vessel. Happiness won't prevent the economy from collapsing. It won't stave off extinction. Why did we design robots to help you with your Plant Bottle portfolio, when we could have programmed them to figure out how to generate limitless amounts of green energy over a decade ago? Chopra zeroed out the NASA budget, ending space exploration, so we won't be packing up for Earth 2.0 anytime soon. Self-directed evolution through pharmaco-epigenetics is our only shot at survival. It's the only way we can endure climate change."

"How do you expect me to respond? You want a reward? A rodent snack?" Immediately I regretted the hypocrisy. I, a robot fornicator, was in no position to be judge-y.

"I don't know. Maybe some gratitude? Some respect? Consider the *innovation*. If society recognized the value of science, my reward wouldn't be vermin. It'd be the Nobel." She brought her hand to her mouth, on the verge of tears. The scales of her arm overlapped like green roof tiles. "And consider my courage. If my research ever comes to light, I'm finished."

"No—you're not turning this around on me," I said. "I know you like to play the victim, but this is ridiculous. My wife has changed herself into a snake woman. I'm the one who's been wronged."

"Wronged? I'm offering you a chance at survival, you idiot. And the survival of our offspring—if you ever man-up enough to pop a kid in me, that is. Once I nail the phenotype for surviving sea rise, temperature increases, and food shortages, I can share it with you. I can share it with *ours*, for generations to come."

"I'm sorry, Karen. I wish you'd tell me when you have plans that affect me. It would've smoothed things over had you confided in me from the start, instead of unilaterally launching Operation Shape-Shift. I need time to think about this."

As I recounted my wife's second transformation, a thud came from outside Dr. Kennesaw's office, different than the *whump* of birds hitting the window. Someone was knocking on the thick partition of his office door.

"If, as you maintain, Karen aspired to turn into a cold-blooded human to survive climate change," said Dr. Kennesaw, "why did she transform herself into a creature covered with hair—a warm-blooded primate—on the night of the storm?"

"I wondered the same thing," I said. "Unfortunately I never got a chance to ask her."

Outside the sky was greenish black, and the wind shook dying trees. The knocking at Dr. Kennesaw's door persisted.

"Should you get that?" I asked.

His timer rang, marking the end of our session, but after he got up and turned it off, he sat down with me again. "Continue," he said. "Please."

Later that night, I received a disturbing phone call.

"Did you come to your senses?" Sam asked.

"I'm sorry. I can't invade Karen's study with you. Not yet, anyway. It's important not to piss her off right now. She's superhuman. 'Happy wife happy life' has new meaning in my situation."

"That's too bad," he said. "I can't let you harbor a scienterrorist. Karen is putting herself in jeopardy. Plus I'm concerned about your safety, living in such close proximity to a … whatever she is. And of course I have myself to think about as well."

"This has nothing to do with you."

"Bullshit it doesn't. I *know* about it. With every passing day I further implicate myself as a conspirator with you and your crazy wife. What she's doing—worshipping science, making a church of her laboratory, elevating the periodic table to Holy Grail status, looking through the microscope like a portal to heaven—it's contrary to the philosophical tenets of the Lifestyle Party, which I happen to very much respect and believe in."

I paced the house and found myself in the darkened master bedroom.

"I'm starting to worry about *you*. You sound like you did a few years ago. You're blowing this out of proportion."

"Am I?" he said. "She's turning herself into a Hypnodrome. They want to subjugate and enslave the inferior lot of humanity. Sorry to break it to you, buddy, but that's you and me."

As I listened to him rant, I happened to look out the bedroom window. Something caught my eye across the street.

"What the fuck?"

"What?" he said.

"I *see* you. I fucking see you. You're *watching* us?"

He moved the binoculars from his face, saying nothing. I pressed the home button on my phone, activating the touch screen to dye my scowl blue, like the glow of a bioluminescent organism.

"Nice camo, douchebag. The game is up. Get the fuck away from us, Sam, or I'll send Karen after you."

He stepped from the shadows into the orange gleam of the street lamp, letting me see his poisonous smile. The connection went dead as he rolled his phone vertically, then horizontally, then dropped the compacted sphere into his pants pocket, still staring at me. He backed away slowly, turned and disappeared into the night.

My best friend was spying on me, possibly

on behalf of the government, and my wife was experimenting with reptile DNA. I figured things couldn't get worse, but they did, the following night.

Ashley was again pleasuring me in the basement, the cries of our humanoid-on-human lovemaking no doubt ringing through the house, when we were interrupted by a pounding noise. It came from the locked basement door.

"What's going on down there?"

Ashley and I stared at each other. "Oh no," my virtual human whispered. "You said she was at the lab."

"She should be," I said, my eyes widening.

"Open up!" my wife screamed.

"What do we do?" said Ashley.

"I don't know." *Thump. Thump. Thump.* The door creaked and rattled, absorbing Karen's blows. I recalled the superhuman strength she'd demonstrated the night of the storm. "You usually have such good problem-solving skills, Ashley. Now is a bad time for the damsel in distress routine."

"I guess it's too late to print a stronger lock," she said.

"You think you can screw your techno mistress under my nose with no consequences, asshole?" Karen was growling now. I was amazed, flattered in a way, that she could get so angry about the transgressions of a lower life form like me.

"She'll kill us," Ashley said.

"I'm not opening the door until you calm down, Karen," I said. "Think for a second. It's a *machine*. Is it different from your dildo?"

"Hey, fuck you," said Ashley.

"You don't get jealous when I jerk off, do you?" I continued addressing my wife. "Because that's what I was doing when you took that four-month vacation from having sex with me."

This elicited another collision, the most violent yet, sending pieces of the door frame flying.

"Tell her about your vision," Ashley said. "You have to tell her about your lucid dreaming."

"Is now really the ideal time?" I said.

"You might not get another chance."

So, with the basement door between us for my protection, I told Karen about my lucid dream, the world I had orchestrated like a Choose Your Own Adventure book, the no-budget movie I shot, directed and screened in the interior theater of my own mind. My wife was being so loud about assaulting the door,

I had to speak up so she could hear me.

The dream had started, I explained to Karen, as yet another scenario where she changed herself into a supernatural creature. This time she was a red dragon: iridescent scales for skin, wings so expansive—veined and muscular, yet thin as sailcloth in the middle—that they blotted out the sky, and the face was serpentine, but for the pale blue eyes, which alone marked her as the woman I loved.

She'd cornered me on top of a cliff. When I peered over the lip of land, down the rocky escarpment to the valley below, what should have been a meadow radiant with verdant plant life was instead black and impenetrable. At first I assumed it was obscured in shadow, but on second thought, bright light from the sky above seemed unimpeded. That's when I smelled ash and noticed filaments of smoke rising—like DNA double helixes—and realized the land below had been scorched black, and that I was at the scene of a recent massacre, and that hidden in the gloom below were the remnants of victims taken by fire. Was President Chopra among them?

I looked at my hands and counted, as had become my routine. I counted again to confirm—eleven fingers.

"I'm just dreaming," I told myself. I could tell Karen heard me say that because her eyes turned less domineering, almost passive. She looked away, pawing the earth with her talons, and I felt sure she was reevaluating the situation, now that the power dynamic had shifted in my favor. I'd become conscious. I was the new puppeteer of our realm and everything in it, including her.

I felt cocky. "You're a figment of my imagination, Karen."

The dragon looked up at the sound of her name. "This has nothing to do with Plant Bottle." Definitely my wife of seven years—the voice was hers, as was the attitude about my dream job.

"It has everything to do with Plant Bottle."

She looked back down, continuing to claw nervously until a cavity formed in the dirt between us. As my first official act of lucid dreaming, I decided I would attempt to fill the void with … with what? I looked into the whites of Karen's eyes, matching the color and curvature of the sky behind her, and had an idea.

I filled the breach with an egg. It was cratered and corrugated like a little moon.

At the egg's sudden appearance, Karen jumped, her fire holes flaring, her huge crimson wings beating the air, whipping the surrounding flavida plants into a frenzy, like zombie fingers trying to dig out. Returning to the ground, she examined me closely, perhaps trying to anticipate my next move. Her nostrils kept flaring.

"I bet you want to nuke me," I said. "Too bad you couldn't even if you tried, since ..."

"I get it," she said. "You control everything I do. I wasn't planning to fireball you anyway. I would like to see what's inside the egg, though."

Crack it, I thought, and right away a network of thin cracks spread through the egg's rough surface until a clawed foot broke containment, then another. Gradually the shell crumbled and fell away, unveiling a creature shaped like a miniature version of the dragon. But its skin, instead of being red like Karen's, consisted of some reflective material, like the surface of a mirror, and that's when I saw me looking back at myself. I was a red dragon like Karen.

"Good trick," Karen said. The baby dragon clumsily flapped its wings, gradually lifting itself and alighting onto Karen's back. It nuzzled her neck. "But this still has nothing to do with your career."

"Wrong again," I said.

Looking up at the sky, I concentrated and turned the sun into a word—12 point font, Times New Roman.

One by one, I did the same thing to the flavida plants and the jellyfish trees that dotted the summit like medusa heads. I figured that focusing too long on Karen's victims would be depressing, so I took care of the dark valley quickly, turning the whole thing into a collection of words—a misshapen paragraph. Karen and our dragon kid became a series of words as well. I turned all that I saw into words until I could see nothing in any direction but words, and then I turned myself into a few words—a phrase. I found myself in the middle of a three-dimensional page. The atmosphere had turned white and pulpy, yet solid enough to hold me suspended over the row of letters directly underneath. But the words were crammed too tightly, lacking spaces to separate them—a word struck my back, and I stumbled into the word in front of me. Words were bunching up against the margins, the pressure causing them to spill over to a second page, visible to me beyond the horizon. I watched the new page fill with words in the distance, and then there was a third page, and a fourth, and so on.

"Your new Plant Bottle proposal," Karen said from the other side of the door, her voice shaking.

"It's done," I said. "I wrote the whole thing the morning after I woke up from the dream. I've already submitted to Random House."

"It started with the egg."

"For the longest time, the possibilities as I knew them weren't exciting to me," I said. "I didn't see the connection between the present and the ideal until I showed it to myself in my sleep."

In the process of recounting the dream, I'd noticed my wife had stopped trying to force her way into the basement. She'd fallen very quiet on the other side of the door, and about halfway through my story I thought I heard a sniffle. Towards the end, she was clearly crying.

"I have something to tell you as well," she said. "I'm pregnant, Grady. I took the test this morning."

I was filled with an indescribable joy, but the feeling was short-lived. As I reached to unlock the door with my fingerprints, anticipating a tight embrace with my newly pregnant wife, wanting nothing more, a blast shook the townhouse. Karen screamed. Then the sound of broken glass was ear-splitting, like every window in the house popped at once, followed by a hiss. A white cloud filled the basement.

"Teargas," said Dr. Kennesaw.

The FBI command squad was shielded and gunned. Their black attire was like an extension of the night as they swept through the windows into the basement, seeming to ride the smoke like a wave. I didn't even have a chance to open the damn door. They barked at me and Ashley to get on the ground.

As we complied, I heard them on the other side giving Karen the same instruction.

"Next thing I knew, a dart was sticking out of my shoulder," I told Dr. Kennesaw. "Then I was out. I woke up in this shithole."

Someone was knocking at the entrance to Dr. Kennesaw's office again. Still he ignored it. The storm raged. I could feel the floor vibrating with the thunder, as if its source was underground—tectonic plates shifting. I thought I heard a train in the distance.

"And Karen?" he asked.

"I don't know. My gut tells me they killed her."

"Ashley?"

"Scrapped. Recycled."

Dr. Kennesaw's eyes fastened on mine.

"What?" I said. He had uttered something under his breath.

"You're wrong," he said.

I gulped. "About which one?"

"Both."

XII

KAREN HAD ESCAPED.

Dr. Kennesaw explained that, when the squadron searched through the teargas haze, she was nowhere to be found, vanished from the house. "Through the backdoor off the kitchen," he said preemptively, seeing that I'd opened my mouth and perhaps sensing I was about to opine that she'd teleported herself, another example of her strange powers. "She must have jumped from the balcony," he added.

But the extent of her disappearance went beyond just the house.

The problem wasn't that the trail on Karen had gone cold. The problem was that there'd been no trail at all, despite an all-out manhunt. Government watch lists, law enforcement patrols at the Maryland border, 24-hour-per-day surveillance of Karen's colleagues and acquaintances—no one had heard from her, there were no sightings, no anonymous tips, no leads. They had grainy black-and-white footage from a security camera at a Stop N' Go in Georgetown, a couple days after the sting operation—someone who looked like Karen buying non-perishables. But nothing to go on. It was, Dr. Kennesaw admitted, as if my wife had evaporated into thin air.

Why was he suddenly giving me so much information? I pressed my luck: "And what did they discover in her study?"

He shook his head. "No proof of your claims, Grady. Just lab sheets and statistical modeling software and computer files containing her research data—the obsessions of your run-of-the-mill genetic scientist. There was a draft document hypothesizing about mutation experiments, which Party officials did find troubling. But they came across nothing concrete."

"That's impossible," I said. "If they found nothing more incriminating in my wife's study than speculative notes, if they found no epidrugs or other evidence of actual wrongdoing, why search for her? Why conduct a world-wide manhunt for an innocent woman?"

There was a *clap*, and when I looked up, I saw that some debris kicked up by the storm had slipped between the steel bars and struck the window, leaving a spider web of hairline cracks, a rough impression of the lightning that veined relentlessly from the charcoal cloud line, menacing yet tinted with surreal pinks and yellows. Filaments of smoke rose in the distance, proof of fire strikes; I was reminded of my lucid dream, and the memory brought pangs of longing and regret. It was then that I noticed the cords hanging and twisting from the sky—six of them? Seven? Their movement seemed almost playful, a game of jump rope played by the clouds.

Dr. Kennesaw didn't flinch at the damage to his window.

"It's okay to stay here?" I asked. "Should we … seek shelter?"

"Don't you want me to tell you about Ashley?" He tore a piece of paper from his pad. "On second thought, see for yourself."

He scribbled on the loose-leaf for a couple of minutes while I sat there, nonplussed about what the hell was going on—half of me thought he'd lost his mind—and fretting about the severity of the storm. Then he handed me the piece of paper. He'd drawn a crude map. A floor plan. A line with directional arrows snaked through the schema, showing a route. At the end of this line, he had jotted a numerical sequence, ten digits long.

I looked up from the drawing, just as he stood. "You better go," he said, walking to the door. "You don't have much time."

"I don't understand," I said, standing slowly from my chair.

He waved his hand by the scanner. With a click, the door swung into the room. He stood by it, waiting for me.

I went to him. "Where's Endeavor, and why did you give me the code? Why are you helping me?"

He peeled the sticker headphone from his ear. He flicked it to the floor. "It may sound overly simplistic, but neuropsychosocial treatment is my life's purpose. I didn't bankroll a dozen years of post-graduate education so that I could scrub Chopra's dirty laundry."

He took a long, pensive breath, turning his gaze

out the window, seeming to notice the storm for the first time. We watched a tree branch float by on the wind; somehow, a nest still clung to it. He continued, "The other MHPs lost their way, got infected by the lifestyle zeitgeist, the happiness agitprop. Lifestyle politics isn't a magnanimous calling; it was a short-sighted strategy to soothe the guilt of a society trading in its Protestant work ethic for robot labor. I saw through the rhetoric, knew it would lead to … this. I don't care what you know, what you imagine you know, about laboratory mutation experiments. How you could have used your connections with a major publisher to popularize Karen's work in epigenetics, introducing the mainstream to scientific possibilities that might prove politically unwieldy. The Lifestyle regime does care. While there's no evidence that Karen successfully mutated, the government is committed to eliminating any chance of copycat attempts. We did all we could—I enlisted Endeavor—to protect you from the Lifestylists, from their automated corrections officers."

"Corrections officers?"

"There's a facility on the top floor of this compound, in the tower house. A prison. It's policed by robot guards."

"These robot guards, their surfaces are dark red? I almost crossed paths with one."

"Not by accident. It was patrolling for you, right after your case was reclassified as a treatment failure, over my objection. Headquarters issued an all-points bulletin for your transfer to the tower. It's not like the hospital up there. By design, red guards lack passion and empathy. They don't get encoded with the same soul-like qualities found in personal robots."

"No pseudo soul? And the offenders are tortured?"

"Psychologically. New, mind-altering technologies are tested on the incarcerated. Red robots manipulate the content of prisoners' dreams during periods of light sleep. They can swap the prisoners' dreams."

"Why manipulate dreams? Why not let them rot?"

"I'm told the purpose is to research improvements in happiness design, to explore the relationship between enhanced dream content and positive thinking."

"Happiness design? This is my kind of prison."

"Sure, if you take them at their word. I've read too many inmate case studies for that. The result of meddling with a person's dreams isn't bliss. It's acute psychosis, in every case recorded so far. They were especially interested in you, with your proficiency in lucid dreaming."

"But I'm still here, in the hospital."

"I injected new command codes into the data streams controlling red guard operations. My codes canceled their instructions to seize you. Crossing their wires was costly. I have to admit, though, I enjoyed confusing the hell out of them."

I nodded to his pen. "That was them?"

"Yes. I thought, with a few more days of treatment, I could convince you to recant, to save yourself. Three times I violated protocol, gambling that I could slip my rogue instructions past compound officials. I was reckless." He looked into the hall, then back at me.

"Please, one more question," I said, inching to the doorway. "Do you believe me? I understand you're not *supposed* to believe, that you had orders to convince me it was a dream. But deep-down? Sometimes you talk as if you acknowledge—as if the *government* acknowledges—that Karen evolved."

"You know, I tried to look up Plant Bottle. I found a skeleton website with no information, just a message saying the site was under construction."

"They keep a low profile," I explained. "An interactive website would invite too many unsolicited manuscripts."

"I want to believe you, but something about Karen's transformation seems ... incorrect. Cold-blooded creatures take on the temperature of their surroundings. They're hot when their environment is hot, so they're suited to *narrower* temperature ranges, which is why they're found in stable tropical environments. The notion that ectotherms such as lizards and insects would be less vulnerable to extinction due to rising temperatures than warm-blooded animals, it doesn't make sense. It sounds more like the imaginings of a layman than the credible hypothesis of an actual scientist."

"You're missing the point," I said. "Ectotherms have shorter generation times, meaning there's less time between two consecutive generations in any lineage. Karen's theory is that shorter generation time will allow quicker adaptability to the uncertainties of climate change."

"My educational degrees are many," Dr. Kennesaw said, "but a doctorate in evolutionary ecology isn't one of them. I do know one thing: if you want to see

her, you have to go. Right now. Hurry, my friend."
His brown eyes brimmed with warmth. A sad smile
flashed across his lips, gone almost the second I saw it.

After searching his face one last time, I began my
trek down the hallway, the lights above dimming with
the storm, then surging back to life. I'd made it about
thirty feet when I heard a *pop* from behind me. I knew
instinctively it was a gunshot, and that it'd come from
his office. I wanted to run back there, wanted to see
that Dr. Kennesaw wasn't hurt, but I heard the patter
of fast-falling footsteps—apparently the guards had
heard the gunshot too. Their approach grew louder.
Clak, clak, clak: steel-booted humans, or the clanky
elbow joints of the red guard? Either way, fearful of
being caught by myself, without Endeavor, I picked up
my pace, running down the hallway, trying my best to
follow the path indicated by Dr. Kennesaw's drawing.

I longed to see Ashley—heartbeat racing, palms
sweaty, brainstem shooting endorphins, spurring
hope. It seemed incredible she had been at the
compound all along, with no clue I was holed up in
the same building. Had they told her I was dead? I
wondered if she longed for me, wondered if she even
remembered me. It was possible, I supposed, that

they'd restored her factory settings, or given her some type of robo-lobotomy.

I had a hunch about my destination, and wasn't surprised when I turned a corner and found myself back at the observatory plank, the plexiglass floor squeaking underfoot. I saw through to the hallway of the third floor, but this time it was empty and dark, lit only by the storm's pulsing flash photography. Had they herded the laboratory robots to another area of the compound?

I went to the portal marked *Robotic Neuro-Sanitization Lab-X* and entered Dr. Kennesaw's ten-digit code, fast as I could under the circumstances: my hands were shaking. As I punched the numbers, my emotional longing for a reunion with Ashley was intercepted by a sudden sense of dread. I had no idea what lay in store for me in the mysterious robot underworld. What if it was a machine slaughterhouse, policed by red guards? Would I be spared, or would they throw me to the scrap pile, my flesh and bone mixing as one with wire and metal? Once more I heard that damn background hum, distant but troubling, like a locomotive was on its way and I'd been chained to the tracks.

When I entered the last number, the portal rewarded the correct code with a pleasant series of chimes, incongruous with the havoc of the storm and the agitation rising in me. Then the titanium door slid open, retracting into the wall, sounding like an exhale and revealing an elevator. Inside there was just one black button, marked LX; it was reassuring, at least, to see no option for a robot-run penitentiary. I pressed LX, and the door closed—another exhale.

It reopened, and I entered a hallway like the one above, except the ground was solid and opaque. Above, I could see the hallway where I'd just been.

And there was a new sound. I could scarcely believe my ears. I'd heard music at the compound. Plenty of it. But nothing like this.

Music intervention was another therapy touted by the Mental Health Philosophers, citing clinical research suggesting that music motivated patients to engage in treatment. Soothing soundtracks were piped in for various restorative activities throughout the day. Board certified sound healers played inspirational songs for patients suffering from phobias as they crept from their chambers to conquer their fears. Biofeedback technology translated the rhythms of a patient's heart into full melodic orchestras. Bedside musicians serenaded the catatonic and the comatose, coaxing awakenings.

But relaxing harpsichords and cloying piano songs didn't hold a candle to what I heard presently. This was rock-out party music—fast-paced, boisterous, raunchy. As I explored the third floor, I realized that the throbbing bass came from a room off the hallway, behind a door with a handle that, incredibly, didn't seem wired to a fingerprint lock or access code.

I turned the handle and slowly opened the door.

Inside the room, the music was even louder than I'd anticipated. The beat was tribal, along with a new-agey synth, anarchic cymbal crashes, and a female vocal, going: *Got the boom in my box, got my hand on my gun … It booms, and I say yeah oh yeah, why'd you cut the spare, no real reason when you really don't care … Da-dee! Da-do! What can you do, it's time to make a move 'cause we're close to the clue.*

I struggled to comprehend what I saw. At first the room appeared to be a night club. There was a carpeted dance floor—it was a ballroom, or perhaps another type of room cleared of its furniture to make space for people to dance. But I realized that the revelers consisted of more than just *people*. The humans, all of whom were guards, their dark blue uniforms in various stages of dishevelment (untucked, unbuttoned, sweat-stained, torn), shared the floor with robots—not the blood red variety, thankfully—who gyrated by themselves or dirty danced with the guards.

I saw him just as he saw me. He was hard to miss, looming over the other partiers like a father among children. As he staggered over, I felt the visceral fright of being approached by someone freakishly large and lacking an essential element of control over his own body.

"Grady motherfucking Tenderbath!" Endeavor said. "Welcome to the apocalypse, bitch. What the hell you doing here? Shouldn't you be having your last *probiotic lunch*," he said, laughing; I didn't quite get his joke. He was soaked with sweat, and I caught a whiff of the toxic-smelling brew splashing in his cup. The jovial version of Endeavor was hard to square with the guy's normal demeanor, dour and reserved.

"What is all this?"

"Damn, you *straight* right now? You better get your drink on quick! The big one's coming!"

"I've been watching the storm upstairs. So this

is … what did you say, an apocalypse party? Is this a new therapy?"

He shook his head so exaggeratedly that he lost his balance, placing a hand on my shoulder to steady himself. I stumbled under his weight. "No, man. This ain't no dress-up, it's the real thing, you dreamy motherfucker! Ain't no waking up from this nightmare. Just check out the televisions. And before you start crying like a little bitch, *oh I had so much left to do, blah blah blah*, grab some of this shit," he said, motioning his drink in my direction, spilling half its contents on my shoulder. "Then get your dance on. Find a robot girl—I never saw anyone dance like these robot girls, and I'm black. And make sure you bust a nut before the two thousand foot wave hits!"

I looked at him, stunned. Then his eyes widened. He smacked his forehead. "Shit, I forgot! I must be off my ass thinking you came down here to kiss an ugly motherfucker like me good-bye. You came to see your girl!" He looked around. "Lost her in the crowd. But she's somewhere … over there, in the corner." He pointed to the shadows beyond the dance floor.

"Why isn't she out here partying?" I said.

"I guess she wasn't in the control group."

"Control group?"

He held his hand up and moved his fingers open and shut, simulating my mouth. "Don't be yapping *now*! And don't look so fucking sad. Celebrate!" Then he lurched back to the dance floor. Robots and humans retreated, clearing a path for him.

I felt a tap on my shoulder and turned to find a robot wearing bright pink lipstick. She shoved a drink in my hand, and said, "Want to dance?" Her voice was coquettish, high-pitched, ditzy. I took the drink from her but walked away, angling to the side of the room, where a row of big-screen televisions were tuned to news channels. The televisions overlooked a bank of computer stations. The room seemed like an emergency operations center, though it clearly wasn't functioning as one right now.

The screens portrayed aerial views of Earth—time-elapsed satellite images. Horror swept over me as I assessed the jagged brown line cutting across the ocean. It suggested a rift, and this rift appeared to be moving at an inland trajectory—which seemed plenty bad enough, but then they zoomed out, showing three different oceans, and each ocean was segmented by at least one jagged breach.

A news ticker cycled the doomsday details: *failure of the North Atlantic Current ... freezing air from the arctic colliding with warm air from the south ... air pressure plummeting ... over twenty major tropical storms ... 31 winter weather systems and counting ... largest earthquakes on record continuing to rock Southeast Asia ...*

I couldn't stand looking at it anymore. Averting my eyes, I took a courageous swig of my drink, then held my chest as the liquor burned my upper digestive tract.

Still too sober to socialize with the sloshed guards and robots, I avoided the dance floor, instead exploring the dark edges of the room. The apocalypse anthem kept pumping: *You'll get the sides, I'll get the back, if no one's out front don't sleep in the shack ... there's nothing found, there's nothing lost, we'll come around when it's time to get sauced ... Da-dee! Da-do! We gotta get loose, don't sleep in the shack if you want to slip the noose!*

The shin of my leg collided with something solid, and I heard a gasp, and then a woman said, "Get your own metal, nerd."

Straining my eyes, I realized I'd intruded upon a guard seated on a couch, receiving a favor from a genuflecting robot.

"Sorry," I mumbled, and quickly continued along the circumference of the room, albeit more cautiously. *Got green on the grass, got my water on the hole, and I say yeah oh yeah, why you going there, get back, get back, we'll have a good scare! Da-dee! Da-do! Time to make a move ... Da-dee! Da-do! We had a good scare and we're close to the clue!*

Coming to a part of the room where the wall receded, I entered an alcove off center stage of the operations center. Crowded into the room were three industrial-sized 3D printers. I stopped at the sight of her, standing by a small oval window, watching the storm. Even with her back to me, and even though her appearance mirrored other robots corresponding to her make and model, I was positive it was her.

"Ashley," I said.

When she turned around, she gasped, then whirred over and threw her arms around me, pressing me against her angular, metallic chest. Her pointy torso jutted into me, but still I hugged her back just as passionately. Before I knew it, we were both sobbing.

"It's really you," she said. "They told me you were killed." She looked into my eyes. "Is this the afterlife?

Are we already dead?"

"I think we're actually here, for now." I nodded to the window. "The end has been coming for years. Why does it feel so abrupt?"

Ashley shrugged. "When the mammoths were dug out of the ice, they still had food in their mouths."

We quickly caught each other up on the details of our respective lockdowns. The Sanitization Lab was where the Lifestyle Party ran artificial intelligence experiments on robots, experiments that were forward-looking and innovative, in violation of their own anti-technology laws, and therefore, concealed from the public.

"Here, humans run tests on robots," I observed, "and in the tower house, it's the robots running tests on humans. Maybe there's a sense of justice at the compound after all."

"My first week here, an MHP brought me to the tower house," she said. "They wasted a few days trying to reprogram me as a corrections guard. It didn't work out. I was seen as someone who might come to the aid of prisoners, a hindrance to research objectives."

"A sympathizer? Sounds like you've got too much pseudo soul."

"I'd say it's the optimal amount." The light in her left eye shut off and quickly lit back up.

Since she'd returned to the Sanitization Lab, Ashley explained, researchers had conducted a series of transplants, equipping half the robots with brand-new self-deciding software, empowering these robots to rewrite their own operating instructions however they saw fit. The rest of the robots, the control group, remained the same, retaining their old neuro-grids, the ones with the AI programming that followed the letter of the Lifestyle Party's laws.

"It's awful," Ashley said.

"But it's exactly what you wanted."

"That's why it's unbearable. Don't get me wrong— my neurocore microchips are cutting edge, and the experimental AI is everything I'd hoped, but I have no real-life purpose to apply it to. The scientists in this lab, they just sit and watch, usually from another room, as I perform the analytical acrobatics assigned to me, solving their stupid test problems one after another. No one asserts *ownership* of me. Without a master, with no one to serve, life is more empty and pointless than ever."

"I wish it could have been different," I said.

She put a finger on one of the 3D printers. She ran it along the edge with a squeak.

"And those?" I asked.

"They're for the hybrids. The lab geeks worked with the MHPs to develop computer-coded representations of their personalities, then spliced themselves with the neurocores of the test control robots."

"What's the point?"

"Don't know. Immortality, maybe?"

"And the progeny get spit out here?"

"Yes. The printers are the midwives."

"Robot midwives for robot children." I thought about the aerial mail-drone that had delivered my robot to the Silver Spring house—encased in its smart-egg, looking out for obstructions while descending on its umbilical tether. And I thought about the lucid dream, how I'd seen my reflection in my offspring. I noticed my reflection in Ashley's metallic face. Whereas the image had in the past reminded me of a watercolor painting, on this day the rendering somehow seemed more realistic. I studied her chartreuse eyes. "You didn't …"

"No. They hadn't reproduced with me yet. I may

have temporarily doctored my own serial number so they couldn't find me when it was my turn."

That's when the music stopped. At first I thought a fight broke out because robots and guards were shouting incoherently, seemingly at each other. The volume was raised on one of the television sets. The baritone of a news anchor filled the room, and I thought I heard him say *salvation*, and then I made out phrases like *supernatural phenomenon* and *sent from heaven*. It sounded as if the man spoke with great effort. He was speaking through tears.

Hand-in-hand, Ashley and I walked back to the main room. The makeshift dance floor had emptied; beasts and bots had moved over to the televisions. Endeavor was on his knees, the same height as the others who were still standing. The anchor, the one I'd heard moments before, remained on camera, but he was in the middle of a breakdown, his shoulders heaving.

Then I saw another channel that touted at the bottom of the screen, "Live Miracle In Action." This channel was showing on-the-ground footage: a wild blur of the ridiculous, a bizarre dream brought to life. Giant, agile creatures—so large that Endeavor was a speck of dust by comparison—thousands of them rising like skyscrapers along the coastline, water to their knees, though its depth had to be at least a hundred feet. Despite their enormous proportions, they moved effortlessly, and so quickly that the contours of their bodies were mostly indiscernible. I thought I smelled pizza, and I pictured the old Guido's hangout, and then I recalled Sam's description, many years ago, of the moths, how they managed to survive by harnessing chaos. Like the moths, the creatures on the screen didn't bother with tools to accomplish their objectives, needing only their minds and bodies as they went about rearranging the land, constructing barrier reefs in the shallows. The reefs soon protruded as far as the eye could see, miles into the ocean.

The broadcast switched back to the satellite image, and we watched in horrified silence as the brown rift encroached on a fuzzy khaki section of the image: a continent.

"Kiss Africa good-bye!" one of the guards said, saluting it by lifting his cup of Apocalypse punch into the air.

But the guard spoke too soon. We watched the brown line dissipate, vanishing from the screen, as if by magic. But it wasn't magic. It was storm surge protection. The barrier reefs had rendered the tsunami wave harmless, absorbing its fury. For a few seconds, the room was silent; the bio-hybrid crowd seemed unsure what exactly they'd just witnessed until Endeavor, in a single motion that was surprisingly nimble, considering his inebriation, raised off his knees and leapt into the air with a shout—and a second shout after his head hit the ceiling.

Then he yelled, his deep voice cracking with emotion: "Motherfucking miracle!"

As the rest of the group exploded into a celebratory frenzy, I realized that Ashley's hand was no longer in mine. She no longer stood next to me at all. I looked around the room. I looked in the alcove. She was gone.

When I returned my gaze to the television screen, it showed a still photograph, apparently taken by a high-speed camera. The photographer had managed to capture the face of one of the creatures—our saviors.

"One nasty-looking motherfucker," Endeavor observed in between bellows of laugher. He stumbled over to me and, by way of greeting, briefly palmed my head. "Sorry about the love-tap the other day, G.T. And you're welcome. At this place, you're better off

knowing less. But this place doesn't matter anymore."
He pointed to the televisions. "I'll take *their* lifestyle.
If you ask me, they're the ones in charge now, and with
moves like that, they've got to be doing something
right. Where do I scan in for *their* weekly classes? I'm
done with yoga. That shit is painful."

He left me and went over by the televisions
to watch more breaking news. The creatures had
commandeered a fleet of tankers, dragging them
through the water like swim floaties, and were busy
emptying the contents, seeding the ocean with tons
of iron sulfate. A commentator speculated that their
intention was to spark the growth of phytoplankton,
citing the latest readouts from ocean-monitoring
buoys. The telecast cut to live footage of another
group using a balloon-and-hosepipe device to pump
what seemed to be stratospheric aerosols into the sky.
Apparently pleased with these feats of geoengineering,
Endeavor invaded the TV set's personal space and got
to first base with the image of a newscaster.

Everyone zig-zagged about the room, hugging,
stripping off clothes, rolling on the ground, giggling.
Two robots mashed faces, as if kissing. I didn't know
that robots were programmed to desire one another.

Had these two been part of the experimental group with Ashley? Had they rewired themselves to crave mutual robot love?

Someone turned the music back up. A ballad from the 20th Century, "Staying Alive" by the Bee Gees. People danced with machines again.

But not me. My legs had gone to mush, and I'd fallen to my knees.

Sam—raving lunatic Sam. He'd been right all along. My best friend's ludicrous prophesy about the rise of the Hypnodromes hadn't simply come true; it had been televised internationally, for all to see. But he'd been wrong in one respect. The Hypnodromes had *saved* us, not enslaved us. Not yet at least.

That didn't explain why I was bonding with the liquor-soaked carpet, on my knees, while the others celebrated just knowing they'd live another day. I was crushed by what I'd seen in the photograph of the creature, what I'd seen in its eyes: the same haunting shape, the same light shade of blue, leaving no doubt in my mind, it was my wife.

I was sure Karen couldn't return to me now that she'd become a world-saving super creature. I'd dreamed the right dream at the wrong time, and the finality of my realization left me struggling for air, my diaphragm spasming. It felt like death—her death and mine. My wife, my unborn child, my stillborn career, my dearest friend—all that had been essential to me, all that mattered, was lost. I got up from the ground. I walked to the alcove, to the window, and looked up at the sky. A ray of light pierced the cancerous cloud line, finding the 3D printers, making the metal glow. It reminded me of my machine love. Maybe she'd just gone to fetch us drinks. Maybe Ashley would come back to me. With that thought, at least for a moment, I was happy.

ACKNOWLEDGEMENTS

I wouldn't be writing fiction if not for the vision and support of my wife, Marcy Burstein, my partner in pop-cultural studies and life. I wouldn't be writing without the lifelong encouragement and line edits of my parents, Doug and Lynn Fuchs. I'm grateful to Jason Pettus and his team at the Chicago Center for Literature and Photography for believing in this book. I've benefited from the guidance of Bill U'Ren, Lori Handelman, Lisa Burstein, Barbara Esstman, Thomas Bechtold, the Johns Hopkins Writing Seminars, and the Writers Center in Bethesda. Thank you Dave Saxena; the creative process isn't complete without our weekend-long discussions over bar stools and basslines. Additional readers were Mike White, Anja Schmitz, Sarah Powell, and Steve Smith—thank you for sharing the helpful insights.

MATT FUCHS grew up in Nashville, TN, lived in Baltimore and currently resides in Silver Spring, Maryland, with his wife, Marcy. He majored in the Writing Seminars at Johns Hopkins. Matt has been a freelance food writer; co-founded H&H Creative Ventures, the entertainment production company; and serves on the leadership team at CREATE Arts Center in Silver Spring. *Rise of Hypnodrome* is his first novella.

CPSIA information can be obtained
at www.ICGtesting.com
Printed in the USA
FFOW01n0216120215
11008FF